MUMBAI MORNINGS

a novel

P. A. CHAWLA

MUMBAI MORNINGS

a novel

Pen-n-Mouse
New Jersey

MUMBAI MORNINGS
Copyright © 2015 by P. A. Chawla
Pen-N-Mouse Press
All rights reserved.

No part of this book may be reproduced, stored in a retrieval system, or transmitted in any form, or by any means, electronic, mechanical, photocopying, recording or otherwise, without prior permission except in the case of brief quotations embodied in critical articles or reviews. Requests for permission should be directed to info@pen-n-mouse.com

This book is a work of fiction. Names, characters, businesses, organizations, places, events and incidents either are the product of the author's imagination or are used fictitiously. Any resemblance to actual persons, living or dead, events, or locales is entirely coincidental.

For information contact: **info@pen-n-mouse.com**

Cover photograph by Chandrakant Seth
Printed on acid-free paper
First Edition: October 2015

Library of Congress Control Number: **2015953964**

ISBN: **978-0-9888221-4-6**

For you Mom always
and
For Najma – no better friend

Contents

Prologue   *1*
Cardamom   *3*
Conduct Unbecoming   *23*
The Daybed   *31*
The Summer I Knew I Was Loved   *43*
The Voodoo Wife   *55*
The Art of Flying   *79*
Swamini   *99*
The Disposable Lighter   *111*
The Swallower of Secrets   *131*
Traditional Music   *153*
The Thief of St. Mary's   *181*
The Homemaker   *203*
Oceanfront Property   *225*
A Murder   *255*
An Explanatory Note   *275*

Prologue

Her eyes said good morning as her hand caressed my hair, making sure I was with her in the flesh and not just a voice on the phone. Often, I wouldn't let her turn the light on or even part the curtains at that sacred hour. Those Mumbai mornings were exclusively ours.

At first, we simply sipped our tea and basked in the silence. Mum seldom asked me about my life in New Jersey. I think not asking allowed her to imagine I dwelled in a sort of paradise where no one ever aged or wept or did the dishes. Then, usually on my second cup, I invoked a name or addressed her past, and slowly she opened her heart.

As she grew frailer, I was no longer content with having her to myself only in the mornings. I tried to spend every moment of my stay ensconced with her in the balcony of our little flat or in the evenings, on a bench downstairs in the children's play area. On occasion, I escorted her to a lunch or a visit to a favorite relative - treats she accepted shyly like a child overwhelmed.

And the stories blossomed. ♦

Cardamom

Words mouthed into a cell phone can sound like marbles clattering helter-skelter down the aisles of a railway carriage.

Words whispered in hallowed places rise above your bowed head, gather the mute prayers of parishioners long gone then spread like cobwebs in the high, unattended corners of old walls.

Ordinary words, spoken out in the open, take on the colors and textures of the day, the warmth of the sun, the merriment of the air, the purple distance of the mountains.

Words spilled from the sickbed are laced with the rank smell of debility. They fill up the room and the spaces in your heart with uneasiness.

Words of love when oft repeated lose their magic, their shine. They sound rehearsed.

Words of unspoken love can weigh you down so that your boots are heavy and life a wearisome journey.

And words flung carelessly in passing sometimes stick like burrs to whoever is closest.

- Saya

I plunged a fork into my breakfast eggs and ate with appetite. The morning paper rested on my right thigh, like a napkin gone askew. I picked up the paper and dropped it aside when I realized I was reading the same short paragraph over and over, like a five-year-old trying to make sense of the Pythagorean Theorem.

My mother raised her brows in amusement.

"Perhaps it is jet lag," I said, by way of explanation.

Travel affects my sleep pattern so that I walk around like a zombie for a day or two, forever looking for a piece of furniture wide enough to accommodate my legs, and when I find it, I stretch on it for exactly three minutes and then bounce back up, wide awake and still un-refreshed. Intellectually, I seem to suffer a bit of lag too. I feel as though I'm looking at the world from a great distance, like an impassioned observer unable to participate in and certainly not liable for events unfolding before my eyes. Why is it we shudder with empathy when we watch the news channel from the comfort of our own couch, but cannot muster the slightest bit of interest when we are abroad? I will never know, just as I may never know why I forego a breakfast of eggs at home but look forward to it daily at my mother's table.

Having demolished my eggs, taking care to blot the yellow crud sticking to my lower lip, I made one last attempt to read the paper. This time I turned to softer news that did not involve defogging the brain matter. I discovered some Bollywood trivia and marveled at the new faces, costumes, and ideas that emerged from the fine print. If there was one thing that could be counted on in previous years, other than congestion and pollution, it was the same set of Bollywood stars ageing comfortably side by side with their audience over the decades. Not anymore. I pointed to this new face or that and my mother, whose knowledge of the industry was as limited as my own, tried to enlighten me. Ah, he's the son of so and so Kapoor, or she is the daughter of so and so Khan. Soon we grew tired of this game.

As I was about to put the paper back into its space above the coffee table, my eyes fell on a photograph I had missed. It looked like a ribbon cutting ceremony for some department store. A glamorous young starlet was smiling into the camera. An assistant seemed to be guiding her hand helpfully toward what was surely an onerous task for one so fragile. It was not the toothy smile of the starlet that caught my interest, however, but the exultant face of a fan almost on all fours like a puppy doing his damnedest to get within an inch of her aura.

"Mum, isn't that Hero Harish?"

My mother sucked her breath in astonishment.

"I did not know you remembered him. It's been over twenty years!" She eyed the photograph myopically and sighed.

"Well, if it is him, I'm glad he is alive."

"What a strange thing to say!" I exclaimed. "Was he ill or in any kind of danger?"

"Ill?" said Mum, who tended to answer a question with a question.

"Yes, you might say he had an illness of sorts, the kind that latches on to your mind and lingers as close as breath or memory."

She slipped into reverie for a few moments, then

sighed, shook herself, and said earnestly, "What I'm about to tell you, Saya, is the story of a young man and how a few careless words altered forever the course of his life."

I held my breath as she began:

> As you know, Harish came here to try his luck in Bollywood films, way back when you were in college. He was not much older than you were, and with his smooth, hairless face and curling lashes that he probably got from his father, he looked younger still.
>
> Speaking of his father, I must give you a little background so you will understand why a conservative, God-fearing man from Jhansi would allow his only son to pack his entire life into a small leather bag and throw himself into the den of wolves that is the Mumbai film industry.
>
> Harish's father, your dad's cousin, Raajan Sahib, started out as a technician in a garment mill. At the end of each day, along with his wages, he was allowed to pick up scraps or remnants of fabric used for women's *kurtas* (tunics), which he brought home to his gifted wife. I say gifted, for not only was she an

excellent seamstress and homemaker she had the ability to create something out of nothing. He often boasted Radha was like the heroine of a fairytale who could spin straw into gold.

And indeed, you saw the proof of her craftsmanship displayed over almost every inch of the house. Patchwork curtains, tri-colored tablecloths and dish cloths, her daughter's little dresses like a smorgasbord of scraps, and even poor Harish was not exempt. He attended his first year of college resplendent in a shirt with a red front and bright green pockets so that he looked like a traffic signal stopping many a crowd of girls sniggering behind him on their way to class.

Yes, she missed the mark on fashion from time to time, but her stitching was flawless. The hem was invisible, the buttonhole the right size, not too big so that the button slipped out, not too snug to make it hard on the fingers, and every dart and pleat and waistband artfully sewn for a perfect, comfortable fit.

Life is not easy for a technician with a growing family. When his young daughter showed signs of blossoming into a buxom young woman, Raajan Sahib, with an eye on the future, counted his savings and found he had just enough to buy a Singer Sewing Machine. He converted part of the kitchen into a sewing area and convinced his wife to create some sample outfits they could sell simply through word of mouth. This idea made her glow with happiness, for it was not often women were asked to contribute to the family kitty in those days, Saya. His wife set to work.

Slowly the business took off. Word spread around the neighborhood like a bushfire. Harish's mother not only charged less than the city tailors, but offered her customers ideas, tea, and gossip all in one sitting. Within a couple of years, Harish's father was able to purchase a little shop on Main Street and then the adjoining one. Soon they were a chain!

Over a cup of coffee, in the City Club one day (yes they could now afford club membership), he heard a woman complain that no matter how hard she tried, she felt lumpy and ungraceful in a sari. "It is these petticoats," she pouted. "They flare out like an umbrella making my hips look big. Wish something could be done." At the time, those were the only kind of petticoats available.

Harish's father could not get the woman's complaint out of his head. He went home that evening, and using the small coffee table as his desk, he drew sketch after sketch with the seriousness of an architect. When finally his wife brought him his dinner, he showed her his sketches and asked her opinion, and soon the two of them were bending their heads together suggesting this and that. It is his belief, Saya, that he was the first to create the pencil-like petticoat that made a woman look curvy and slim in all the right places. Of course, ordinary housewives did not care for this style and only wore it on occasion because it required them to walk with small mincing steps like Japanese women in kimonos and was not very practical.

My point is this. As the husband and wife team got more and more involved with the designing and tailoring business, a new, sophisticated clientele began dropping by.

Instead of tea in glasses, the ladies were now served with china and seated on comfortable, cushioned chairs. Full-length mirrors, wider fitting rooms, and high-powered lights lent a sort of opulence to their little shops on Main Street. Even his wife, a naturally beautiful woman who had taken on a sloppy, neglectful air over the years, began to spend a little more time on her toilette so that the air around her now smelled of sandalwood and scented oil. The locals began to feel more like smart city shoppers and congratulated themselves for not moving out of the area now that the differences between city and small town were narrowing. Today a smart tailoring shop, tomorrow a three-star restaurant and a movie theatre, they thought optimistically.

But it was the visit from the actress Shazia that has to do with my story. It is what really led to the chain of events involving Harish and his future as an actor.

The actress Shazia emerged from her white Chevrolet (considered very prestigious in those days) and stepped into the tailoring shop, skirting around a dog pile as delicately as a princess. Raajan Sahib, seeing the famed actress resplendent in white and gold, turned pale with excitement, and it was all he could do to stop himself from bowing and kissing her hand like a lowly vassal.

Harish, who seldom visited the shop, (it reminded him still of the mortifying days of the red shirt with green pockets), happened to be around because he had forgotten to collect some tuition fees he needed that morning. Cash in his pocket, he was on his way out when he all but collided with the petite Shazia.

Shazia was at the height of her career in those days. "You do remember her, don't you, Saya?"

She was pretty cocky, a real tease. "Oooh, watch your step, young man. Your muscles will crush me," she said, winking at him.

Then she asked his mother who this young man was who looked like a handsome hero of the Indian screen. Harish's father, who for one absurd minute thought it was to him that she referred, simpered and wiped beads of perspiration off his shining forehead.

His mother covered her face in embarrassment and Harish turned the shade of beetroot. He forgot he had to run back to college to make his payment within the hour, and instead, in a rare moment of inspiration, opened a bottle of cola and offered it to the actress.

"Thank you, Sir," she said with mock servility. "And if you are ever in Mumbai look me up. I need a hero like you desperately." And with those words you might say, a star was conceived.

Shazia stood in the center of the shop quite unselfconsciously to be measured for petticoats in all the colors of the rainbow. She then asked to have them delivered to the film studio on the other side of town where she was shooting.

"You won't run off with one of my 'extras' if they come to your shop, will you Hero Harish?" she winked, nudged his biceps, and tittered as his cheeks burnt like the flaming sun.

Harish did not pay his college fees that year but used the entire amount for a new wardrobe, a pair of pointy white shoes, and some close-up photographs taken at the only studio in the city.

He then sneaked the photographs inside the folds of the petticoats custom-made for Miss Shazia and awaited her response. If there was a part of him that feared Miss Shazia was merely playing with him and would likely look confused at the pictures and throw them in the nearest bin, he quelled it easily. He was young, passably good looking and utterly enamored by the "Hero Harish" moniker. He imagined the morning paper lighting up the city with a full-page photograph of Harish and his bulging biceps: Handsome hero of Bollywood. Why not?

He did not hear back from Miss Shazia.

But his mother did. Miss Shazia invited her to set up shop in Mumbai, promising her a steady amount of business, so pleased was she with the new, figure flattering petticoats.

I did not know at the time what hoops Harish had to jump through to convince his parents he could make it as an actor, but he was here one day knocking on our door expecting us to give him room and board, as if we did not live under a city roof barely large enough to shelter our own six bodies. It was only years later that we discovered that his parents, equally enamored by the charismatic Miss Shazia, had also packed their bedrolls and left, soon after Harish, for the city lights. They did not do too badly as it turned out. Miss Shazia kept her promise as far as the tailoring went and did give them her business. In fact, Harish's father, now known as Raajan Sir in the film world, became the head costume designer for Shazia and many other movie queens. Ironically he even appeared in cameo roles in a few films as himself, measuring a woman's waistline or bust line and generally behaving like a fool I am ashamed to say. But I'm afraid all his film contacts did nothing for Harish. He was treated as the tailor's son and invisible outside the context of his father's shop.

"Then did he just give up?" I asked, a little disappointed.

"Give up? No. Not for a long, long time. There are many twists and turns, a few ups but mostly downs in Hero's story, Saya."

"He was young at the time, and the idea of

seeing himself larger than life on a big screen took hold of him like a leech. In fact, a leech merely sucks one's blood, but all faith and no powerful backing can suck the very brain cells of one so callow!

"A new upcoming starlet, catching sight of his lashes curling over his sad eyes, befriended him and, you might say, became infatuated with him. Somehow she convinced a producer to have Harish come in for a screen test, promising the old man whatever it is that women of loose morals promise. After his screen test, he was so excited I thought he would burst open and spill adrenaline, like a watermelon split in half. I asked him quite casually what exactly he had to say or do at the screen test, and he gave us quite a demonstration."

"Oh my God, the cardamom story!" I shrieked and clapped my hands.

"Yes," Mum confirmed. "The cardamom story."

He had to lend expression to the word cardamom in as many ways as he could. By the end of the afternoon, everyone was rolling on the floor laughing at his acting:

Cardamom? - A solicitous question.

Cardamom! - Pleased surprise.

Carda ... mom - Sigh of disappointment.

CARDAMOM - As in ordering a servant.

And so on.

He was too excited to notice our hilarity and did not take offence even when the story of his "acting debut" spread like wild fire in the building, and kids, servants, and random neighbors began addressing him by his new name, Cardamom, from then on.

Something did come out of the screen test though. He got a twenty-second role in the starlet's next movie as a face in the crowd, one among hundreds watching a cockfight in a village! He could not understand why we appeared so underwhelmed after we paid good money to watch the movie. Now, I feel sorry that I was not more encouraging. Harish was starved, foraging for recognition. How ignoble to deny a hungry man a piece of bread.

After that film, Hero Harish, so grateful to the producer for giving him screen time, became the man's full-time, unpaid mentee. I do believe the producer was fond of him in a paternal sort of way. Harish probably reminded him of the hardships he himself had to endure before someone took a chance and gave him a break. Also, he was touched by the naiveté of the boy. So eager was Harish to maintain a connection, however dubious, with the film world, he was willing to run around all day serving endless cups of tea to the assistants of set designers!

And another thing... despite being in an industry that seems to do its best work when the shadow is longest and the dark deeds of men surface like scum on still water, Harish preserved the sanctity of his body and soul, never chewing tobacco, drinking, smoking, or visiting the floozies who left their doors unlocked during the night. For the producer then, Harish became a sort of moral compass or a shining example of small town values or some such thing. After a couple of years, however, the strain of not succeeding was getting to Harish. Your dad did not want him to visit us anymore because of the way his eyes would light up when he looked at you, Saya, and his own father threw him out because Harish caught him in a back room of a film set with his hands on Miss Shazia's hips and his head buried in her ample breasts.

My mother shook her head in wonder and continued:

How little it takes for even a good man to forget his values, his religious training when the Shazias of this world roll their kohl darkened eyes. Although Harish did not utter a word, Raajan Sir could not risk having his wife get a whiff of his transgressions and found a reason to pick a quarrel with the young man when he arrived home late one evening. This Harish confessed to me in a weak moment when he was hungry, homeless (his film-world friends would not put him up anymore), and desperately in need of money.

He flailed his arms and legs like a drowning man and survived somehow, taking part time jobs distributing flyers, painting banners, promoting videos, and finally, utterly at the end of his wits, sold his soul for a few notes in the bank. I'm not being dramatic, Saya. He started by scalping movie tickets, then became an assistant for a photographer who made depraved, X-rated films - you are old enough to know what I mean - and last I heard he was pandering!

My mother shuddered and wiped her eyes.

"So he never settled down, never married, I mean?" I asked, studying his picture closely again.

"Oh, did I not mention that?" Mum asked.

As a matter of fact, he did get married way back when he was still that producer's apprentice. I suppose the girl's parents took into account only that Harish's father was a man of means, well settled in the city, and assumed they would surely help his only son support himself. Anyway, the intelligent young bride soon realized he was in no position to support her and took to visiting her parents for months at a time. At least, at her parents' home, she would have a sure roof over her head and a safe haven for their little one, who came exactly nine months after they tied the knot. Each time she returned from a visit, her parents gave her, as is the custom, enough cash and jewelry to tide her over until the next visit.

When Hero Harish went underground – he was in some deep trouble that I can only guess at – she finally took it upon herself to run the household. As I said before, she was a smart woman with a degree in education. She began teaching in a convent school and did reasonably well for herself. I believe she recently bought a one-bedroom flat on the seaface.

"Do you want to know where she got the money for an apartment like that, Saya?" asked Mum, arching her brows when she saw my look of disbelief.

"Her son is a child star. He's been working in at least three films a year for the past six years that I am aware of. How is that for an interesting turn of events?" Mum looked at me in triumph, aware she had my attention.

I took one last look at the faded black and white Harish scrabbling through the anonymous crowds. His face and upper torso jutted forward, his legs hidden in the tangle of spectator limbs, his one hand stretched longingly like an impoverished follower of Christ in a biblical painting at the Museum of Modern Art. There was desire yes, but also a vacancy in his eyes. He was a man chasing not so much a dream, but the memory of one, I thought. Perhaps a glamorous Shazia sequined in white and gold, fueling his nascent fantasies, slithered timelessly, ceaselessly into the skin of the star du jour - a Rani, a Kajol, a Kareena - winking at him from afar, come join me Harish, you handsome hero of Bollywood! And Harish, like a stuck tape, tripped exactly at that moment, letting escape from his fingers a tuft of stardust.

On impulse, I cut out the photograph and stuck it into my scrapbook along with the obituary news clippings of people who'd passed through my life over the years. There he lies still. ♦

23

Conduct Unbecoming

Maybe the bride-bed brings despair,
For each an imagined image brings
And finds a real image there.
> **- William Butler Yeats**
> **("Solomon and The Witch")**

"Did you sleep well?" asked Mum, brushing my hair with her fingers.

"Yes, although I kept dreaming about Hero Harish. He

seemed to be in some sort of maze from which he could not find his way out."

"I should not have told you the true story about him. I don't like to see you disturbed," Mum sighed.

"Oh no, Mum. I'm glad you did. Besides, with truth comes understanding. You have always taught me that."

She sighed again and changed the topic. "So what has my *beti* (daughter) planned for the day?"

What I really wished I could do was rediscover the city with my girl pal, strolling through the narrow gullies of childhood, reminiscing about this and that, mindful of every step as the path curved, caved in or regurgitated splinters of glass, cigarette butts, prawn shells and banana peels, depending on the nervous and digestive habits of the inhabitants of the building towering above that patch of land. Instead, I was nagged into accepting invitations from relatives from my mother's side on my first week home.

"Aunt Veena," I reminded her with a sour look.

"I'm sorry you have to cancel your outing with your friend," said Mother, "but I sort of promised Aunt Veena and Mad-dog Mahaan you would drop by for lunch."

She then clapped her hand to her mouth in embarrassment.

"There, you see!" I exclaimed. "You call him Mad-dog Mahaan too! Surely that's not his given name?"

"Of course not." She hastened to explain, "There's a story behind it."

I looked at my watch. The telling of it would cut into the time I'd agreed to spend with my youngest aunt, but that did not bother me one bit.

My sister-in-law came in just then and with a gleam in her eye, volunteered. "I can tell you if you are really interested," she said, and when I nodded eagerly, she began:

> Before he ever met your aunt, Mad-dog Mahaan lived on the seventh floor of an apartment building called Tower Heights. He cut quite a figure in those days, tall and slender, his pants tight as second skin, a silver buckle gleaming like an obscene invitation on his pelvis and a yellow muffler around his neck that he believed often reeled in the ladies. But there was no dearth of roadside Romeos in his neighborhood, and Mad-dog was not quite as successful as he would have one believe. Often, on rainy days, he sat on a wicker chair in his enclosed balcony sighing and staring at the

setting sun and nursing a glass of black tea, his muffler drying on the laundry line above him.

Then one day, just as he began to despair he would dry up like a prune before he found the woman of his dreams--a cross between the reigning Indian actress Madhubala and the French Brigitte Bardot no doubt--he heard a hum in the air that quickly changed to a warble and, at last, into a full throated crescendo, and within the space of a verse, Mad-dog Mahaan found himself in the throes of love. Mind you, he could not see the singer. He knew only that the notes rose above him, and that it was a female instrument that peeled those silver bells, transporting him to the gates of heaven where he quivered like a sitar player before his muse. What made it even more enchanting was that it was a new song, a modern song, a ditty that he was convinced only a young, chaste woman with a potential for passion could sing.

Mad-dog-Mahaan did the only thing he could. He answered the singer with a tune of his own.

Days turned into weeks. All night long Mad-dog Mahaan invented tales of torrid romance between a young knight and his lover with the voice of an angel, and all evening he sat in his balcony singing duets with the woman he privately called his nightingale.

Why, you may ask, did he not walk to the apartment above and simply introduce himself?

It was not very easy in those days to get permission to visit women, though it was part of his plan. But for once, the roadside Romeo was a little afraid and wanted to be sure when they met that she would fall into his arms without preamble or protest.

At last, one evening, when he sensed her singing matched his own in fervor, he could take it no more. Mad-dog walked the fifteen steps to the floor above, rang the doorbell, and awaited his fate.

A comely girl, about sixteen, answered and spontaneously put a hand to her cheek. Mad-dog saw her velvet skin turn from pale peach to delicious red as she met his eyes. He immediately stammered his love. Wide-eyed and dumbstruck, the silly girl followed him out the door and to the beach, skirting around neighbors and curious eyes. There they sat and held hands and watched the sun go down.

After that night, there was no point wasting their evenings apart from each other. Now they met behind every hidden nook and cranny that could support their weight and behaved like lovers everywhere.

One day, when the sun looked more gloriously orange than ever, the wind teased his nightingale's hair and his yellow muffler looked especially bright in the evening light, Mad-dog whispered to her to sing him his favorite song.

"Song? What song?" she asked.

"You know very well, the one you sang with so much passion…that evening seven weeks ago."

"Mahaan, are you OK?" she giggled. "I never sing. Not even in the shower. It is my sister who takes voice lessons."

At first, Mahaan thought she was joking. He insisted. "Anything," he pleaded. "One line."

She hesitated, tried a few notes, and stopped

when she saw the look on his face.

Mad-dog fought for air. It was as if he had drunk a cup of paraffin oil and was about to choke out his last breath. "You are not my nightingale!" He shook her shoulders.

She emitted a small scream.

"Shut up!" he whispered.

Afraid and repulsed, she whimpered and tried to move away.

Perhaps it was *her* revulsion that he could not accept, considering it was he who felt cheated. It is understandable, is it not? Take the dream away from the dreamer and what is left ... a life of gestures? His face was very close to hers. Mahaan inched even closer, and with a phlegmy little growl, he sank his teeth into her left ear lobe and chewed it right off!

Blood spurted out of her ear and oozed down her neck. She sprang up and fled from the scene, screaming in terror all the way to the apartment complex.

"Who did this to you, Miss? Who hurt you?" the watchman asked.

"It was Mahaan. That mad dog! Someone should have him shot!" she shrilled.

"And that is how he got his name," Mum interceded when my sister-in-law couldn't stop giggling.

"So what did they do to him? Anything?" I asked Mum.

"For unbecoming conduct? Not really. He was ostracized by the building adults for a while but forgiven in time. The girl was sent away to relatives until the gossip died down, and her ear healed. I believe she needed stitches. Only the name stuck, as you know --Mad-dog."

Now Mum too covered her mouth and giggled like a child. I shook my finger at her in mock rebuke and made my reluctant way to my aunt's. ♦

# The Daybed

And so we hobble to the finish line with rasping faith and spasmodic bouts of loyalty.

- Dina

With Aunt Veena's visit thankfully behind me, I planned to fly to the South the following week, this time to pay my respects to my favorite and eldest aunt. I took a deep breath and invited my mother along, giving her ample time to get used to the idea. What followed was a flurry of activity on her part: a visit to the dentist to get her dentures to stay fastened, an inventory of the grain bins (I've no idea why), and squabbles with the laundry boy who over-starched her outfit so that it lay stiff and unrelenting as a floor mat and would have to be rinsed and re-ironed in time for her to pack. I realized, of course, it was simply anxiety playing itself out and wisely stayed out of her hair every time I saw the telltale creases on her forehead.

Keeping up a steady stream of chatter, I took my mother's ice-cold hand and stroked it gently to stop the trembling. When the flight took off, and she was settled with her glass of juice and peanuts, I wondered aloud if anything had changed at all in my Aunt Dina's house.

"Does she still sit cross-legged on her daybed situated strategically at an angle from the door, always partially open so she can see everyone who passes across without being seen herself?" I sniggered.

My mother looked at me with reproach.

"It is not by choice that she sits there, Saya," she said.

Then looking into the distance and shutting the door on the present, she told me this story, the years dropping off her face:

> When her husband was among us, your Aunt Dina did not even own the daybed. Her place was next to him in the largest bedroom, the one

overlooking the children's park.

They had a perfect relationship those two, or at least I thought so. When he talked, she listened, and when she talked he had better listen if he knew what was good for him! They stood as equals, Saya, at a time that society sanctioned, even proclaimed, the inequality of women, and although he loomed over her like a blimp, if they ever butted heads, it was he who ultimately bent his in quiet assent.

I have a photograph of the couple that I will someday share with you. She is looking ahead as if surveying her kingdom, her head uncovered, her veil resting lightly on her shoulders; but it is the expression in your uncle's eyes stealing a glance at his bride of thirty-odd years that gives him away. When you see that picture, Saya, I am sure you will be moved. Plenty of photographers use up their film on young lovers. Of course, youth has its appeal, more so because it is so fleeting, I think. However, it is a rare artiste who can capture so eloquently the love between two mature people who have faced the highs and the lows, the madness of summer and the dreary predictability of the monsoon, together and with equanimity.

That is not to say that they did not argue like two old codgers, those two! He snored, and she sighed. He demanded an explanation of household expenses, and she pleaded a headache; he loved his sweets, and she hated his excesses. And one night, tired from quarreling over a movie they had to interrupt because of the way he chewed his popcorn in the dark and the embarrassing flatulence that followed, she turned to face the wall and ignored his tentative advances. It was the last night they spent together as a couple in that bedroom.

For a few minutes, my mother did not speak. History unspooled before her eyes leaving her subdued and shaken. Then she resumed:

Early next morning, she turned to face him, surprised he hadn't left for work. Your uncle was an early riser and often the one to wake the servants for morning tea. Fumbling with her glasses, she sensed that he seemed too still and rather oddly positioned. She tried to rouse him, and when he did not respond, she uttered a little scream bringing in her daughter, several grandchildren, and two servants to the room. By pushing him this way and that, clutching his wrist, and pressing an ear to his chest, it was declared he was alive but in need of medical attention. Of course, he was hospitalized. Your aunt tells me, for days, even in a state of coma, his body would shake spasmodically as if trying to escape, furious at its own helplessness. He was diagnosed as having suffered a stroke at some point during the night. To this day, Dina curses herself for not having noticed anything amiss. I tell her perhaps she was very tired and slept undisturbed since for once he did not snore or make repeated trips to the bathroom.

Your uncle never did recover from the illness that tied him to his bed. Dina nursed him day and night. Then one day, exhausted to the point of delirium, she rested her head on the living room couch and got a maidservant to keep vigil at his bedside for the night. A week later, her daughter bought her the daybed despite her protests and convinced her to retain the night maid. Like me, your aunt is parsimonious by nature. After five long years of being shackled to his bed, your uncle passed away. That dear, dear man!

I adjusted the overhead fan to give my mother time to compose herself. She was weeping silently now, but she never liked to appear weak.

"Anyway, soon after they cleared the bedroom of his effects, her eldest grandson announced his engagement," she said.

"They postponed the formal ceremony, of course, until the appropriate time. Meanwhile Dina found she could no longer enter the bedroom that had been filled with her husband's presence for forty years. She had the place painted a soft lilac, arranged to have the old bed re-upholstered and brought in a spanking new steel armoire and an expensive Kashmiri rug. When it was finished, she bequeathed the area to the new couple, who was thrilled. Ever since, your Aunt Dina sits, sleeps, visits, and orders the servants from the daybed in the living room."

The plane landed the moment she finished reminiscing.

A short while later, we were at my aunt's doorstep breathing the welcoming aroma of cheese fritters and samosas. I greeted my aunt eagerly, astonished as always that she looked so much smaller in person. I believe the feeling is not unusual, for often one tends to confuse stature with status. I know I certainly did.

After the obligatory samosas at the dining table and her affectionate scolding, *"How thin you look! What ails you child?"* we moved toward the frayed living room sofas.

"Why, Auntie Dina, how is it I don't see your daybed anywhere?"

My mother too looked surprised.

My aunt rose to her feet then and said with a mischievous smile, "You want to know what I did with the daybed? Come to my room."

"Your room?" Mum and I said in unison.

Completely befuddled, we followed her in. It just so happened that her grandson was finally able to afford moving into his own apartment, giving the lilac bedroom a momentary look of unshared air.

"I was aware that my other grandchildren longed for the room. After all, the young really covet their space, don't they? But after so many years of sitting on that daybed like a passenger in the waiting room of a railway station, I thought it was time I moved back to my own room."

She looked at us somewhat defiantly.

"Of course, you did the right thing," my mother assured her. "It is just that I thought you had grown comfortable and rather enjoyed being at the center of things."

"Ha!" said my aunt.

"I admit, Jaya, it was my idea to move out of my own room when he passed away. But imagine for a moment how it feels to have all your belongings in a cardboard carton tucked under your bed, out of sight from visitors, and within reach of prying servants sleeping virtually at your feet! My children speak about quality of life, of club memberships and weekend outings, and fresh mountain air for a mere sinus congestion. Do you know what my idea of quality of life is? A cubby for my slippers, a hanger for my scarf, a shelf for my hairbrush and night cream, a drawer for my underclothes, and just for once, the television situated at an appropriate angle so I don't have to get a crick in my neck whilst viewing."

With that, she fell silent, overcome with emotion.

"Well, I am so very happy you have your bedroom back," I said after a suitable interval. "You were very generous to give it up for this long."

"Now, you have place for all your things," Mum added.

"Yes. A place for everything and everything in its place." My aunt smiled in a satisfied sort of way and brushed the TV monitor with a rag.

"And I see the daybed is here!" My mother sat down, gesturing to us.

"Yes, it is where I sleep still."

Now we were truly confused. She gets back her enormous custom-made bed, a canopy of mosquito netting billowing over it like soft dreams, and chooses not to sleep on it!

She simply stared back at us, her eyes wet.

"You find it hard to sleep on the bed you shared with him?" my mother finally whispered.

She sighed deeply and replied, "The first night

I moved in, I was so happy I did not sleep a wink."

Years ago I'd shared the space in the armoire with my grandson and his wife but soon the drawers bulged with their clothes, t-shirts, skirts, and whatnots and I felt squeezed and finally out completely. So I took the time to press and arrange my clothes neatly in an organized fashion. Then I lined the storage shelves with some left over wallpaper and displayed my sandals side by side like in a store. I put my linens, starched and folded, in one drawer and towels in another. It was wonderful!

The trouble began on the following night and every night thereafter. I rested my head on the great double bed, but for the life of me, I could not sleep. I felt nauseous, light headed, like a little goldfish used to floating about in its small tank and suddenly flung into the high seas! I moved to the far corner and faced the wall, and for a while that was better. But then I heard sighs and grunts and felt a dipping in the mattress as if someone was trying to get comfortable beside me. I rose with a start and turned on all the lights. I can do that now, in my own room you see, without worrying about waking up the servants. That helped a little, but, of course, with the light in my eyes, I could not sleep. Then one night as I hugged my arms and prayed silently for rest, I distinctly heard *his* voice.

"Come, Dina, let's go. Let's be together."

We shuddered collectively.

"He loved you very much," I said, more to fill the silence so laden with unsaid things than to make a point.

"What did you do?" my mother asked, her eyes round with fear.

"I sat up and waved a finger at the air."

She gestured dramatically to show us how.

I said, "NO! I DON'T WANT TO. GO AWAY!"

Then I moved my pillow and bed sheet to the daybed. He hasn't bothered me since.

My mother and I, mindful that a careless word could cause her pain, made no comment.

My aunt lifted my chin, looked deep into my eyes as if

seeking a verdict, and then enunciated each word carefully, "I had a good marriage, a good life, but this is what I'm used to now. And I want to live." She released my chin letting her hands, balled into fists, fall softly onto her lap.

Her words sizzled like corn just before it pops in the oven, then bounced off the bare walls, and echoed in the room:

"I WANT TO LIVE!" ♦

The Summer I Knew I Was Loved

I must have music. Through music, He reveals himself.

- Jaya

We stayed with Aunt Dina, much to her disappointment, for only two nights. "Why is your visit so short?" she scolded.

She insisted on walking out with us all the way to the

street where she waited until we found a cab. I apologized profusely and promised I'd try to visit again before I left. She nodded resignedly. Of course, we both knew that wouldn't happen.

On the flight home, I watched my mother recline on her seat, her expression calm and sated like a child who'd received both nourishment and a bedtime story, and contentedly shut her eyes. Soon however, turbulence and a flurry of announcements woke her. She opened her eyes and gazed at me with that inexplicable look reserved for daughters. I caressed the fading marks of small pox that had taken away her childhood and said, "No one can tell you ever had these. They have faded almost entirely."

My mother sighed and shook her head sorrowfully. "The pox may have faded, but the memory of it never does."

I was sorry I brought up the subject and sought to change it, but she went on:

> Until the age of eight I was considered a bit of a beauty, you know. I was given preferential treatment by relatives and friends alike, and the most expensive silks were reserved for my frocks. I wore velvet slippers embroidered with gold and fashionable scarves and baubles on my hair. A lady servant oiled and brushed my

hair each night and washed it with scented soap the next morning.

Then one summer I got sick. Our mother had long since died (during childbirth), and my father remarried the woman who became your grandmother. She came from a desperately poor family, but she was young, beautiful, and motherless herself. She helped raise us children efficiently, but soon had children of her own and found it difficult to spread her love fairly and well.

Anyway, when I got sick and not simply with measles or mumps or any such ailment that one can put behind and even bring up easily in conversation years later, "Remember the time so and so got sick," but with this dangerous disease, I think she almost lost her mind. She was afraid the contagion would spread and take one of her little ones. Well, I survived, and thanks to her care and vigilance in keeping me quarantined in an upstairs room, the other children stayed safe. That was a lot of alone time for a small child like me. Solitude can be sweet when you are tired or in love or retiring for prayer; otherwise, Saya, it is unnatural, like a yearlong December pressing ice to your heart.

When I recovered and felt strong enough to look into the mirror, I scarcely recognized myself. The scars stood out like proof of evil - savage, venomous, and permanent. I did not think I could feel more fear and pain, but I was wrong. The attitude of friends, relatives, and most importantly, your grandmother changed overnight. I was no longer the radiant, privileged child of Shri Ramdas. I was a pariah, a wicked creature who would now have to earn love. I remember how hard I tried to make her smile. A word of praise from her helped me get through the night.

Being an observant and bright child, I soon realized that it was not my fluency in languages, my poetry recitations, or my lilting singing voice she cared to hear. But occasionally, when I dressed my younger brothers and sisters, helped them with school work, set apart the ripest fruit for their tiffin, saving the bruised fruit for jams, and made the beds before I left for school, she would throw a crumb at me.

Some little tidbit, not directly, but within my hearing, addressing the servant, "See how well she did that. You can learn from an eight year old." Those were the moments that I craved, and when I received them, I rolled them in my mouth and chewed the nourishment like a beggar forever unsure a morsel may come his way again.

One day, your grandmother was more short-tempered with me than usual. It seemed I had used more than my share of hot water in my bath, and the servant had to heat some more. This meant the children would be late for school.

Furious and within your grandfather's hearing, she said, "All the hot water in the world will not improve your looks now, so why bother?" And as if that was not hurtful enough, she muttered, "What a fate to be burdened with an ugly girl child."

I still feel the pain the way a healed foot relives a fracture every winter.

Then your grandfather stood above us; he was a very tall man, nearly six feet, red-eyed, and breathing hard. I tell you, Saya, I was so afraid I thought I was going to wet myself, but for once, his anger was directed at her. I remember his words as if it was yesterday: "Don't forget, Tara, this daughter was named after the Goddess of Wealth. Disrespect her, and you are disrespecting the Goddess herself." Then he glared at me to stay out of sight and marched out of the room.

I don't know whether it was superstition or fear of her husband's wrath, but she did tone down her thorn-like comments from then on and contented herself with either averting her body as if repelled by the sight of my face or darting poison-dipped looks in my direction.

The following summer your grandfather arranged for me to visit an aunt in a city called Sialkot at the foot of Kashmir. This aunt had a heart full of love and no children of her own, and often begged to have one of us visit.

I cannot say, Saya, that I felt loved again, because I had never known a mother's love to begin with. My aunt looked at me as if I was a fairytale princess and understood my needs before my saying so. She fed me with her own hands and rocked me in her arms if I so much as scratched myself with my own short nails. I admit I found every excuse to be petted, embraced, and sung to sleep. Which is not to say I forgot my duties. As soon as I realized she had no servants and undertook all the chores herself, I began helping out. I swept the porch and peeled the vegetables. I folded clothes, dusted furniture, watered her plants, and polished my uncle's and my own shoes. The soft tears and hugs I got in return, I can say without exaggeration, were worth their weight in gold.

My mother sighed and sipped her juice.

"What about your uncle? Was he nice?" I asked.

"Ah! A true saint. Let me tell you," said mum, "unlike my wealthy father, he had a small income and worked as a clerk in a government office, but his was a rich, a generous heart."

One day, he took me to the city shops, asking me every few minutes, "Surely you want an ice cream? A toffee?" Sensitive to his position, I declined although an ice cream in that summer heat would have been heaven!

Your granduncle was well known in that little community and stopped often outside this shop or that one to chat with street vendors. One owner excitedly told him how the street had been flooded with carts the previous day and vendors with boiling cauldrons of some strong smelling brew they called "Kofee" had tried to convince everyone to taste it. Apparently, it was all the rage with the British Sahibs.

"How was it?" asked uncle.

The shopkeeper screwed up his face. "Bitter, bitter mud colored stuff you need to lighten with milk and drown in sugar before you can drink it!" he said. "It will never sell."

Little did he know coffee would become as common as a morning greeting.

I stood quietly waiting for him to finish his story, shifting my weight from one foot to the other when the morning breeze carried with it the sound of an instrument so sweet it made my eyes sting. "Let's go there, over there," I pulled at uncle's *kurta* (tunic).

Amused, he followed me down this lane and that and finally said, "That is a residential street. The music is coming from someone's home. How can we go there?"

But I wouldn't listen. I needed to see for myself the sorcerer who could evoke divinity with a string. We found the source of the music at last and stood outside a partially open door sprayed with cheap blue paint. My uncle somehow managed to invite himself in, and the gracious musician allowed us to sit and listen to his ragas for about an hour.

At the end of it I said, "I need to learn this instrument as well as you. Please teach me."

The musician was quite amused and told me, I would need a sitar and would have to practice twice a day for the rest of my life in order to be any good. I turned away then and walked out the door. Asking for things involved drawing attention to oneself.

"But you do play the sitar. I've seen pictures," I said.

"Indeed," Mum said, and continued:

> A few days later, it was time for me to return home. My aunt held my face as if memorizing each feature and wet every one of my scars with her tears. How loved I felt, Saya, and how bewildered. What was it about this disease-ridden face that caused one woman to open her arms and another to thrust it out of the way?
>
> At home, everything was the same. Your grandmother wasn't in when I returned. She was at the temple. A servant gave me my lunch.
>
> "Promise me, Saya, for as long as you live, when your child comes to visit, you will greet her with a smile and a hug. Show her how cold your home is in her absence and how she warms your heart."
>
> Anyway, two weeks later I came down the stairs to find a casket-like trunk in the living room. Your grandfather beckoned me with a smile and asked me to open it. I looked at your grandmother. She nodded assent. Not daring to breathe, I did as he asked. "Read the note

first," Grandfather urged. I read it once. Then once again.

"A small gift for the one who loves music from a man of small means. May she find God in it. Lalaji (this is how he addressed my father), please don't return it. I beg you."

I looked at the trunk. There wrapped in muslin and lending voice to my deepest longings was the finest sitar, a sitar fit for an empress!

"I have arranged for music lessons for you. You will start tomorrow," said Grandfather, that wise, benevolent, king of a man.

Mother felt silent, so caught up in the exquisite memory, I could almost see the years drop like a veil to reveal a rosy faced child with piercing intelligent eyes mutely expressing her gratitude.

I looked down at her hands. Her index finger stroked the air unconsciously; her head swayed to the sweet rhythms of memory. Her eyes were shut, the lashes curling, fetal-like. I could not help thinking of the mystical princess Mira and how she expressed her lifelong devotion to the Lord with poetry and song, when Mother interrupted my reverie in a voice trembling like a note in the wind and said,

"The year was 1936, the summer I knew I was loved." ♦

The Voodoo Wife

I am not strange. I am simply alone.

- Shanti

Just one short visit with Auntie Dina and my mother looked so happy. Her smile was a gift I wanted to keep forever, so I constantly devised ways to make her smile. The following day, I convinced her to accompany me to Morning Raga, a movie about the fusion of classical Indian and Western music against the lush background of a village in South India. I knew she would love it.

We emerged from the restful dimness of the movie theatre into the lashing heat of the summer afternoon. I held her elbows gently, afraid as much for her as for myself. Neither of us relished the idea of being assaulted or trampled underfoot by the excitable crowd.

The worst of the tugging finally behind us, we stood for a moment catching our breath. From the corner of my eye, I noticed with satisfaction that while she looked a tad disheveled, her eyes still held that beatific expression only classical music could inspire. I was glad I'd selected that particular movie and felt my skin tingle with happiness.

Poking my head this way and that, I was trying to hail a taxi when I felt her fingers digging into my waist in a fearful way.

"Let's go that way," she whispered, almost hurting me now.

"What is the problem?" I asked impatiently and then stopped as a woman grinning in a wild sort of way pushed herself out of the crowd and careened to a halt so close to my face she almost skimmed my nose.

"It is you, isn't it, the daughter from America?" she shrieked as if she'd discovered gold in a trash can.

My mother's arm was now wrapped possessively around my shoulders. "Yes," she said, "and we were just leaving. Oh, there's the taxi."

She whisked me out of sight before the woman could say another word.

"Well, Mama, that was kind of rude." I shook my finger at her.

She didn't reply but sank back into her seat with a sigh. "Are we going home now?"

"Certainly not," I replied. "You are not cooking today; we are going for Chinese."

I directed the cabbie, above my mother's usual soft protestations, to an upscale restaurant.

"Now, tell me, why did you not want me anywhere near that woman?" I asked after we'd discussed the menu at length and ordered the inevitable Sweet corn soup, Vegetable Lo Mein, and Manchurian chicken.

"Saya, did you not recognize her? That was Shanti, the "voodoo wife." You didn't think I was going to let her sink her talons into you, did you?"

I laughed aloud at her words. "Oh, I remember her now. Does she really practice voodoo? And why would she harm me? In fact, she seemed eager to get to know me."

My mother joined her hands as if in prayer and raised her eyes to the heavens. "God forbid."

Then she allowed herself to be served her soup, picked up her spoon, and said, "Now Saya, everything I tell you, you should take with a pinch of salt. After all, these are fragments recovered from one relative or another and pieced together to make sense."

"Relatives? You mean the Sister Network?" I grinned wickedly.

It was common knowledge that she and her five sisters chatted constantly, letting neither illness, geography, nor the cost of long distance calls get in the way of their daily huddle. She smiled serenely and began:

> Shanti was the daughter of a prosperous grape farmer from Nasik. She was an only child, which is rare in a household where the firstborn is a girl, as you well know. Her mother, however, was a sickly young thing and warned by the family doctor that the burden of another pregnancy might be too much for her to bear. Assessing the situation, the farmer decided to plod on without sons, although a

feeling akin to destitution clouded his heart. He showed his resentment by moving his cot to a room at the back of the house overlooking his vineyards.

But things are never as simple as they appear on surface. The walls between their separate beds ultimately caused a rift in their marriage that widened with each passing year. For not only was he depriving his wife of their weekly conjugations but breaking with tradition, the nightly habit of adjusting this way and that to make room for the other and the subtler pleasure of waking together as friends, equals and householders.

He was a poor sleeper, I am told, and would often sit on a lounge chair in his porch, smoking cigarette after cigarette, watching in turn the shooting stars and the fireflies that ignite the night for one intense moment and then disappear forever like all earthly pleasures.

As for her daughter Shanti, the first nine years of her life flew unremarkably by in that verdant valley of the grapes. Supervised by servants, she grew up physically strong and self-possessed, but with very little of the tender attentions usually accorded an only child. It did not occur to the mother to disallow a male servant from bathing or dressing the child or taking her away for day trips to the city when he ran errands on his bicycle. Perhaps that is why the sense of shame or self-consciousness about one's body, so ingrained in young women, was simply foreign to Shanti.

Anguish, bitterness, and a mad anger against her husband burned in her mother's heart. She was a woman of appetites, in the prime of her life yet discarded like a grape seed by her man. She took to roaming the woods alone, mile after mile, ranting and muttering imprecations, grape juice trickling down her chin, letting herself in some time during the night, drunk with tiredness. But sleep would not come.

Time moved on. Shanti was due to have her tenth birthday. She decided she would have her entire school of twenty-four children spend the day with her. Most of her friends were grape pickers' children and rather poor, but the way Shanti looked at it, the more children she invited the better her chances for presents. Her father agreed to help her set up a picnic in a clearing by his vineyard. Even her mother got into the spirit of the day and ordered the servants to prepare the child's favorite dishes.

"You can have fruit and drinks outside, but the main meal should be indoors. The kitchen is large enough," she said. Shanti, thrilled to get her mother's input, readily agreed.

She had just left an invitation at the house of her father's head gardener and was in fact trying to swing his rickety fence door shut when she heard an argument from within.

"Why do you want our child to go to that black magic woman's house? It is not safe."

"She is your boss's daughter. What could I say?" came back a sharp retort.

Shanti heard the words but could not make sense of them. Her heart raced as if she'd been climbing uphill; she understood only that her mother was being cast in a bad light, maybe even an evil light, and that the voices behind the fence had something to do with the troubling dreams that often roused her, shaken and afraid, in the middle of the night. The nubbin of anguish in her throat made it hard for her to swallow. I must get to the bottom of this, she thought, running down the dirt road, through the vineyard, past her father's window and around the front. By the time she clambered up the front stairs, she'd made a decision. What made it that much easier was the fact that school was out, and it was the first day of the holiday season. From that moment onward, she decided, she would become her mother's shadow.

My mother paused to finish her soup and then waited in silence as the waiter served us our main course. I asked for a bottle of water. When he left, she resumed:

When you grow up in a village unfettered by footwear, jewelry, and fussy clothing, it is easy to follow someone like a cat, without attracting attention. Also, her mother, having no reason to believe her activities were of any interest to the child, did not care to look behind her as she went about her errands. Then again, she was the mistress of a vineyard and had long since taught herself to conduct herself as one, her head held high, her back contemptuously stiff, her skirt held up lightly on each side with thumb and index finger to avoid the pits and bird droppings along the streets. It was only in the woods, where she thought she was completely alone, that she let loose her harangues.

Shanti saw her mother take off for the woods on a Monday. She followed her, the sound of her heart drumming "badgirlbadgirlbadgirl" until she learned to ignore it. Her mother was walking faster and faster. She was quiet, not chanting or picking grapes and stuffing them into her mouth. She just walked purposefully toward something or someone. She stood for a moment behind a tree. Three trees behind, Shanti hid as well.

To her horror, her mother pulled down her panties from under her sarong and flung them to the ground. Then she walked toward the hutment of the village priest.

Shanti tiptoed toward the hutment also, not daring to breathe, avoiding every twig like a confession of sin. She was tall enough to peep through the dirt opening that served as a window. But should she dare? Even a child growing up in a village knows one must not invade the privacy of adults. Somehow she got past the "badgirlbadgirlbadgirl" sound rising to a din and looked within.

I will not go into the details, Saya; you can very well guess what was going on in there. Shanti dragged her legs back home, made her way to her bedroom, and fell into a slumber so deep she did not wake until the following morning.

She willed herself to follow her mother from afar for four more days. What she saw was a woman given to chanting, wailing, gathering roots and herbs, squeezing out a white milky liquid from some wild plant, and gathering it all in up in a little black cloth bag embroidered in red and green, and fragments of glass woven like omens in the fabric. One might argue that her mother was merely interested in medicinal plants and their effects on her own constitution. But take into account her secret forays with the priest in the woods, her "mindless" rants that could easily have been mantras, her husband's separate sleeping arrangements -yes, the servants talked- and it was easy to understand why the villagers thought her strange and carelessly labeled her the black magic woman.

That evening, Shanti made her way to her father's side of the house and sat quietly beside him on the porch. If he thought this visit unusual, he did not say so. A gold cigarette lighter and a pair of binoculars lay between them.

Shanti picked them up. "What is this, Father?"

"Binoculars."

"What does it do?"

"It brings things that are far up close."

"And what about the things that are close? Can it make them go far?" she asked.

Her father looked at her with a sad smile.

"No, Shanti, human beings do that all by themselves."

Shanti picked up the binoculars and looked through them. She sucked in her breath. A couple of washerwomen were bathing in the pond on the far end of their vineyard. They did not have their tops on. Beads of water glistened on their fat, purple nipples. She put the binoculars down and went back indoors.

"Will there be anything else?" the waiter asked in a tight-lipped sort of way.

My mother shook herself with a start. "Are we sitting here too long?"

"It's a restaurant, Mama. We can stay as long as we like." I asked him to bring us coffee and ice creams, mango and pistachio flavors. He went off as if given the monumental task of rolling a rock uphill.

Mum continued with her story:

> The next day, Saturday, was her birthday. The day dawned clear and cool. The school students showed up, the servants set up the games, passing around scarves for the three-legged race, gunny sacks for the sack race and so on, not to mention balloons to pop, lollipops to suck, and sugary drinks to keep them hopping. Her parents sat side by side separated only by their thoughts.

Shanti watched as if from afar, taking in the props designed for happiness, even the weather joining in the farce, and thought it was just as well the servants looked so joyful, for although it was her parents who gave her life, it was the hired help who made it livable.

The time came for cake and presents, and with a practiced smile, Shanti thanked the grape pickers' children for the colored marbles, the handmade wooly toys, and the teatime toys. The head gardener, pushing his daughter forward, gave her a bunch of pink ribbons loosely wrapped in a scrap of newspaper. Shanti's face, white as a sheet, crumpled before their eyes. In a voice at once loud, brazen and trembling she said, "I don't want your present. Please take it back." The gardener put a hand protectively on the shoulder of his child. Shanti's parents jerked their heads up. "Shanti, how dare you insult your friend?"

The entire school body was staring at her. A servant stopped in the middle of picking his nose to warn her with a glare.

"I don't want her stupid ribbons." Shanti's voice

was filled with tears. She felt the pinch of her mother's fingers even before they squeezed her ears.

"Apologize, now!"

Shanti looked at her mother's forehead shining with perspiration. Her father stood behind her, holding his temper and steadying his wife with one hand on the small of her back. Perhaps she saw the irony, her parents brought closer together by her bad behavior, joining forces against her.

"They call you Black Magic Woman. They all hate you!" she shouted at last and fell to the floor, kicking and screaming and carrying on like a child.

All I can tell you is the party split up very quickly after Shanti's outburst. The sequence of events after that is a bit hazy. Her mother went to her parental home for a prolonged visit, but in fact it was the last time Shanti ever saw her. Her father confided to an aunt that it was impossible for a man to raise a growing daughter alone, and the aunt agreed to raise Shanti like her own if he promised to look in from time to time, implying of course that he would replenish the family coffers for her trouble.

That is how Shanti found herself in a seedy little apartment in our big city.

"Did she blame herself for her mother's decision?" I wondered aloud.

Mum shrugged. "So much happened so quickly."

She was now stuck in an apartment with six other human beings. They spoke big-city language, full of hidden meanings and colloquialisms, wore big-city clothes, colorful with matching shoes and sashes and bows in their hair and brought in their friends who snickered behind their hands at the girl from the village. Shanti stared at the sea of alien faces around her and surely felt trapped and helpless. Outside the window, the ocean snarled and writhed like a living creature, and she could not tell where it came from and where it was going. She looked at it and her slight frame rocked like a paper boat drowning rapidly.

The village had been her world, as neat as a checkerboard crisscrossed with grape trees: there was her house and there was the temple, humble and small and designed like a cave, sitting diagonally across from the kitchen window. There was the road you could bump along on a bicycle. Continue on this road to get to the city shops and beyond that to the great river Godavari where you could take a dip on holy days. They said even a hen, knocking about that village, could eventually find her coop. And now it was gone, disappeared like her mother, disappeared like the fireflies that have no use for the city.

Did she miss the silent presence of her father etched against the evening sun, binoculars in his lap? Did her heart ache for the mother walking companionless, a prey to "god-men" and her own imaginary demons? Despite her confusion, I'm sure she did. They were her parents after all, her introduction to the world, and when they disappeared, her landscape changed forever.

Bit by bit Shanti began to make a life for herself.

Back in the village, she had studied in a one-room school of twenty-odd children. When she first stepped into Saint Leo's, she felt like a little calf bracing herself to be gored by a militant herd. More than sixty children to a classroom, about eight hundred boisterous children in one stone building. She kept her eyes to the ground at all times, her footsteps crunching on the gravel. The debris and the occasional clump of leaves gave her a sense of solidity, of being closer to the village earth.

They say you can tell a person by the company he keeps. In Shanti's case, there was no company. She was lonely and kept to herself at all times. Of course, it was not really possible to be completely alone in the apartment. The entire family shared one bathroom, and at night, Shanti had to share a small cot with a girl cousin whose inappropriate touching made Shanti increasingly uncomfortable. As she got older, being around people still made her head swim. She angered easily and even became violent, so she was left alone, and that did not help I suppose. Like her mother, she became secretive. She would rise at dawn when the city was still. Only partially awake, she walked for miles. More than once, a servant spotted her behind the cemetery, which was probably the only green spot left in the city, talking and singing to herself. An ignorant and superstitious man, the servant began spreading tales about her morbid interest in the dead. It was not long before she was dubbed "voodoo girl" by the locals.

"Ah! So that's the story," I said and looked around for my waiter.

"Not quite," said Mama.

"Your Uncle Raj met Shanti quite by chance. He was invited to a party in the same building where she resided. Out in the balcony for a quiet smoke, he was about to stub out his cigarette and carelessly fling it below when he spied her. Perhaps she had a feeling she was being observed and looked up reflexively. Later, he admitted he felt as if a bolt of lightning struck him. Shanti was tall and dark, with a serious face, but in her eyes, there was an intensity that could be quite mesmerizing, especially for a young man. Lately, too, she had taken to lining both her lids with a dark pencil so that her eyes looked enormous. To make a long story short, they were married at the end of the year. If your uncle heard whispers of her strange ways, he ignored them. And when her father, at the engagement ceremony, put in his new son-in-law's pocket a check large enough to buy a vineyard, not one member of the family felt inclined to voice their misgivings.

Shanti adjusted surprisingly well at first. Although she moved into a joint family dwelling with four of her husband's brothers and three sisters-in-law, as well as his parents, it was a well-planned bungalow, and she loved it. The cool stone floors, the high French windows, her room overlooking an empty lot instead of the ocean, which she still feared, she couldn't have asked for more. But your uncle travelled a lot, and once again, Shanti was left to her own devices.

She enjoyed her husband's attentions when he was around and for his sake tried to befriend the family. The one brother who was still single became her sometimes companion. They

> played cards, and went to an occasional play and now and then she even asked him for a cigarette "for fun." As for the other wives, she simply did not mingle with them. She would not cook, had no interest in sewing, and did not care for the movies, dramas or gossip that filled their days. They tried to include her at first, and then interpreting her lack of interest as arrogance and standoffishness, they left her alone and later became openly hostile.

The waiter hovered over our table again. I paid the check and urged my mother to use the bathroom before we took the cab home. By the time she returned, I had hailed a cab and held open the door for her. She got in with a sigh.

"That was a good movie and a delicious lunch," she said.

I smiled my thanks and implored her, "Now, finish the story."

> The girl Shanti, a name so unsuited for one who was seldom at peace, brooded incessantly. She felt deeply insulted and conspired against. It hurt her too that the elders of the family, her husband's parents, did nothing to make her feel comfortable. One day, listening behind a door,

she heard the words "voodoo wife." Suddenly she saw her mother's face, wild-eyed and reproachful, and realized with a shock it was really her own in a hallway mirror. There was no way to tell exactly who all were in that room, giggling and gossiping about her, but I think their words burst open the floodgates of her rage, and she swore she would destroy the happiness of every woman in that household.

She was not her mother. She would not "lose" to the gossipers and disappear, leaving pain and dread in her wake. The role of aggressor suited her much better. From then on, she began spending her time with self-professed swamis, learning rituals of all sorts. She collected herbs, roots, powders, and potions from quacks. She visited the cemetery after each burial and the crematorium after each cremation. What she did there is anybody's guess.

It was at breakfast one morning that one of the sisters-in-law complained about her tea. It tasted rather strong. As making tea was Shanti's job, she could barely manage anything else, they all looked at her.

"It's good for you," she said sweetly. "There's basil and ginger in it, very healthy." If the women noticed the men were being served out of a different pot, they didn't think it worth mentioning.

Mind you, these events took place over twenty years ago, but a couple of weeks of that morning brew, and both the sisters-in-law and the elderly mother took to their beds and have been chronically ill with some disease or the other ever since. Shanti, radiantly healthy, took charge of the household by default and drove them like horses, with a very long whip! Quite an irony, don't you think? The girl who did not want to be like her mother made similar rumors about herself true.

My mother shivered visibly.

"How did the men handle all of this?"

My mother looked at me as if trying to make up her mind about something.

"Tell me!"

She whispered, perhaps afraid the cabbie might hear,

"It is rumored she invited them to her bed and does so to this day, and they go to her without hesitation."

Then she looked at my face. I thought I was going to gag.

"She has maintained her looks, Saya. Still lines her eyes, is healthy, fine figured. And the other women, they have so many health issues, one no longer knows whether it is the illness or the medications that keep them bound to the sickbed. Under the circumstances, I suppose men will be men."

I thought about that remark offensive on so many levels.

"And the brother who wasn't married at the time…?"

"He never did get married. They say he is completely enamored by her, sways to the snake charmer's flute."

It was my turn to shiver.

"So now you know why I whisked you away from her, Saya. She's a bad influence!"

My mother held my hand again as if afraid. I paid the cab and opened the door. "Voodoo Wife!" she breathed and held her shawl closer.

I was helping her out of the cab when the watchman

came panting over to us. "Madam, while you were out someone came to your home."

"Who was it?" Mother asked.

The man scratched his head miserably. "I can't remember her name. You were not in, so she asked me to tell you: You are invited to dinner with your daughter from America."

Then his eyes lit up. "She said she'd just bumped into you, about an hour ago."

Mother and I looked at each other. "We were at lunch an hour ago and did not meet anyone, did we, Saya?" she asked, innocent as a child.

"No. No one at all," I said with a straight face.

"Next time, please remember the visitor's name," she chided gently and stepped inside the elevator in her dignified way. ♦

The Art of Flying

And when I run out of things to buy, will I then have it all?

- Ritu

My mother was ill. It was her belief that Shanti, the "voodoo lady," had somehow made her sick. I told her she was surprisingly superstitious for such an intelligent lady, and it was very probably the restaurant meal that had given her indigestion.

Anyway, she had mild nausea, fever, and general

weakness. Too early in the day to worry really, but it was disquieting nevertheless. We insisted she stay in bed, and she agreed willingly, a sign that all was not well, for she was a woman who equated rest with laziness and being still with death. Even now, as I stood watching her in sleep, her eyelids flickered, her sitar fingers fluttered, and her toes flexed and curled to some discordant music playing in her head. I pressed the back of my hand lightly on her proud forehead. It felt hot. She murmured and shifted. I took her hand and pressed my own face to it. She opened her eyes and looked at me with a sweet, lost expression.

"It's your daughter," I said.

"You think I don't know that? Only a daughter can love me so." She smiled. I was glad she was coherent. Surely it meant the fever was not too high? I suggested cold compresses to bring the fever down.

She shuddered, "No, I'll be all right."

"Maybe some tea?" I asked hopefully.

"No dear, nothing. Just stay with me."

I nodded and took her hand.

Three days later, the fever finally broke. She let us sponge her and help her into freshly washed and ironed clothes. She sipped some buttermilk and ate a few spoonfuls of a rice and lentil concoction. The color returned to her cheeks, as did her feisty spirit: *These curtains need changing. The blanket smells funny. The floor looks unwashed.* Ordering the maid was her way of being in the loop and controlling her universe.

"You have a visitor," I told her one day." I'll bring in some chairs, and try to forget the curtains for a bit," I teased gently and showed in her sister Harini.

Surprisingly, Mum didn't look too happy to see her. I'd always thought she was really tight with her sisters. I flitted in and out with the customary tea, cookies, sandwiches, and so on, but the air was fraught with tension, and they sat without making eye contact and merely exchanged inanities.

"What was the matter with Harini Auntie? She barely spoke a word to either of us," I said after she'd left.

"Don't let it bother you. *We've* done nothing wrong," Mum said defensively.

"Has *she*? Done something wrong I mean?" I asked.

My mother shrugged and flicked her fingers suggesting I let it go. But after a while, she asked, "Do you remember her daughter Ritu?"

"Of course. Poor Ritu. We were close for a while. You

know, Mama, I never really learned what happened. How did she die so suddenly?"

My mother took her time answering. "I will tell you, since you are old enough to know, but it's a long story."

I smiled inwardly. Great, telling it would serve as a perfect distraction. I pulled the chair closer.

"Ritu was the youngest of five children as you know. By the time she was sixteen, your Aunt Harini had both her sons well settled abroad and two daughters married. I'm sure she was financially and emotionally quite exhausted. It is not easy spending on college for all your children plus the two dowries and one looming over your head."

"Dowry!" I exclaimed. "They still ask for that?"

"No, they don't ask, but they still expect it. I thought you understood our ways," my mother shot back a little tersely.

I let it go, and Mother told me this tale:

> After high school, your cousin Ritu insisted on applying at the College of Commerce not so much because she had a head for economics but probably because she liked the idea of commuting to the other end of the city, far from spying relatives.

Ritu was still in the first year of college when her father passed away, leaving Harini in a state of shock followed by deep depression. Somehow, Harini had always thought she would be the first to go, with her diabetes and angina and what not. For months, she would not stir from bed, letting Ritu entertain herself with television and the videotapes she received from her brothers. She had not yet blossomed or learned the art of being pleasant and had few friends. I know you visited to keep her company sometimes, Saya, but you had to change buses twice to get to her house and had to discontinue because we did not think it was safe. Of course, her sisters rallied around at first, helping with the house and their mother's bouts of crying but sooner or later they had to return to their own husbands. The best they could do for Ritu was to offer her small presents as if she were not a child in need of comfort but a house pet who could be satisfied with the occasional treat.

For her first year-end function, Ritu had an outfit created, coincidentally, by your father's distant relative - Raajan Sir of Bollywood fame.

I'm not sure if that got her any attention in college, but as she squeezed herself into the train compartment, she felt several eyes boring into her artfully designed cleavage. It was then that she noticed with a start she had jumped into the gents' car. A quite understandable occurrence during the evening rush, I suppose.

"There is room here at the back. You should sit down," someone ordered rather than suggested. Dutifully, she negotiated her way to the end of the crowd and sat down beside the tall, wiry looking man holding a seat for her.

"Thanks. I thought I was going to suffocate," she muttered, quite pale with the effort. And that's how she befriended the notorious Mr. Mahwah.

Somehow, he managed to convey to her that he was an eminently successful movie producer forced to take public transport that day because he had generously let his assistant borrow his car as part of an elaborate treat for his girlfriend. Ritu found his explanation, given with an indulgent smile and befuddled shake of the head, quite charming and did not notice the grey hairs poking out of his chest. Maybe she was not intelligent enough or simply too absorbed in other matters to realize that she seemed to bump into him more and more often. When a chance meeting turned into coffee, then a movie, and soon a day's picnic at a nearby resort is anybody's guess. But soon, I am sorry to say she was embroiled in a torrid affair with a middle-aged man of extremely bad repute.

My mother paused. It was an old story, but she looked visibly upset.

"Maybe you should sleep now," I said. "I'll hear the rest later."

She nodded and sank back onto her pillow. Soon she shut her eyes and snored in her ladylike way. I switched on the fan, making sure to keep it at low speed, the way she liked it, and went into the kitchen to make myself a snack.

She rose in time for her four o'clock tea and cream filled biscuits. After I cleared the tea tray, removed the extra sheet twisting under her legs, and plumped and raised her pillows, she sat back and picked up the story anew:

In my time, and I'm not saying those were better days, just different, the idea of spreading your wings and learning to fly off to college or a career and so on just did not happen. A girl went from her parents' home to her husband's, naïve, introspective, and unschooled in the ways of the world. Ask any mother of daughters today and she will tell you this: the years following high school and before marriage are the most difficult ones. You have to be eternally vigilant, watch not only a daughter's comings and goings, but also inspect the flush on her cheeks, the brightness of her attire, her appetite, her periods, her taste in music, her need for privacy, her reading habits, and even her urge to use the toilet at odd hours. Do not look so shocked, Saya. All mothers do this preventively, covertly, and round-the-clock. But so wholeheartedly did Harini embrace her grief over the one who was gone, she neglected her duty toward the ones still present, and the result is before you!

Ritu was not quite a girl, not quite a woman. Her body was changing every day, making her squirm and itch before she became comfortable in it. There were days she bloomed like a rose, and whoever caught a whiff buzzed in admiration. Then there were days when her skin broke out or she happened to wear brown or her hair got temperamentally frizzy, and she felt dark, ugly, and unloved. She disliked the attention of roadside riff raff and then sulked because not a single boy whistled or made inappropriate gestures when she went by. She wanted to be known as sensitive, intelligent, and as giving as Mother Teresa, but she also wanted to be seen as elegant, sophisticated, and sexy like Marilyn Monroe in high heels and red lipstick. She carried around her beloved True Romance comics, but hid them between the pages of Shakespeare and Tagore. And underneath it all, she greatly missed her father, one of those rare men who paid attention to daughters. I guess, what I'm saying is, she was a little lost and finding her way.

Mum gestured for her flask of buttermilk and drank thirstily. I thought she was being a bit judgmental, but I held my tongue.

And into this simmering pot of contradictions, entered Mr. Mahwah with his silky ways, pulling out of his hat every magic trick known to the seducer, to tease, coddle and flatter an innocent girl into submission.

From being open and forthright with her mother, Ritu became a sly, secretive young thing. She began staying out late and then later. When questioned, she simply shrugged and implied she had been visiting one sister or the other. Harini believed her, perhaps because she wanted to, and because it was convenient. Things went on like this for a while. But it was not enough that the man used her in every way possible for his own evil pleasures; he had to ruin her completely.

One day, he invited her to a movie premiere. Never having been to one before, Ritu was so excited she was nauseous.

He asked her, "What will you wear? This is an important event, a very glamorous event."

"Perhaps I'll borrow something from one of my sisters," she said.

Mr. Mahwah looked skeptical. The next evening he bought her a gift. It was a long, red, slinky dress, low at the back with sequins and stones on the bodice. When she tried it on for him, he looked so exaggeratedly besotted, she knew she could not refuse his present, expensive though it was. After the premiere, where she was completely agog over all the film star glamour, he took her to a fancy restaurant and bought her steak and potatoes and some other fancy fare she was not accustomed to eating. When she looked confused, he smiled and cut her meat for her with his own knife and fed her like a child. Then he patted her head like a father and let her sip several glasses of wine out of his bottle.

On the drive home, she needed to make a bathroom stop. He stopped the car in an obscure street, walked her behind a tree, pulled down her panties, and let her pee as he held her. You see, he gave her whatever he thought she needed at the time until she was full to overflowing with drunken happiness. Finally, he dropped her at her mother's doorstep, his one hand lingering over hers, loath to let go, begging her to come with him to a party the following weekend. She had the presence of mind, even at that point, to ask with arched brows, if she would need another fancy outfit. He said she would, and he would buy her one if she agreed to come. She agreed. Ritu was indeed spreading her wings and planned to fly so high she would soon be unreachable.

"Mum, how could you possibly know all these details?"

"Well, Ritu could not live with the secret of her affair without sharing with a single soul, and those confidences made their way to us in the form of letters."

Intrigued I leaned in, and she told me the rest:

Ritu decided to make a confidante of a girlfriend in England and wrote her long, revealing letters. I think she had some misguided belief that people abroad were more broadminded and would think nothing of her transgressions.

A stack of correspondence tied with orange string arrived with a cover note to Harini saying she was a friend of Ritu and that what probably began as a lark seemed to be morphing into something palpably evil. She said she feared for her friend's safety and must warn Harini that her daughter was in way over her head. After giving the matter considerable thought, she was sending all the letters she'd received thus far, putting responsibility where it belonged. She said she hoped Harini would be able to stem the fire to their reputation with the truth now before them in black and white. All the details were in there Saya, but what was so unfortunate was the fact that the correspondence, postmarked fifteen days *before* Ritu's untimely death, arrived, thanks to our mail delivery system, five days *after* her demise.

As I said, Mahwah had invited Ritu to a weekend party, and she agreed. Even Harini did not generally approve of overnight visits, but Ritu convinced her mother everybody went on overnight college picnics these days. Besides, it was girls only. She was getting increasingly adept at deception, you see. She knew instinctively that as long as she kept her stories simple and interspersed with just the right number of safe words such as *sisters, college, library,* or *girlfriends*, her mother would probably stop listening midway through the conversation and give her consent.

What transpired during that and many such weekends, one can only imagine. This much I can say: Ritu was skittering down a slippery slope and not a caring hand in sight. I'm sure it must have been a heady experience at first, a glorious sense of freedom, being released from her mother's self-confinement, her sisters' housewifery, and her brothers' indifference. To return home after even two nights away must have been boring and anti-climactic! Ritu found fault with everything. Their furniture lacked taste, her mother's cooking was bland, she had outgrown her books, her friends were childish, and college courses so meaningless. She tried going out with her classmates, showing them make-up tricks and introducing them to the musicians who seduced with innuendo and song, but they were wary of her and her fast life, and she was a little afraid of their direct questions. So when Mr. Mahwah began calling more and more often, she sank gratefully into his willing arms.

The young may scoff as much as they like, Saya,

but there is something to be said for the benefits of sleep and custom. Without sleep, you lose the shine in your hair, the life in your eyes, the radiant glow of youth, and certainly your composure. And without the hood of custom, you become vulnerable to the elements and the filth and contamination that ultimately seeps into your soul.

Poor Ritu became addicted to a different, bawdy sort of music, a wild drummer. It destroyed her rest and made her greedy for more. Then we heard she was taking a trip to Paris and another to Dubai and one to Hong Kong, no thanks to the fiend who backed her like a racehorse that was his personal investment.

One day she asked for another dress in her pouting, girlish way. Curtly, Mahwah said he couldn't get her one. Ritu was shocked to say the least. That same evening she noticed his eyes devouring another young girl who looked fresh and ripe as a mango. He did not make any overtures, but certainly his mind was elsewhere, and Ritu felt the first spark of fear

> spike up her back.
>
> On the way home, she was quiet.
>
> "Is something wrong? Is it because you still want a new dress?" he asked.
>
> "Yes," she answered.
>
> This time he told her how she could get one.

I swallowed this sordid bit of information silently. In the meanwhile, my mother nodded off briefly and then came back with a start, for the upstairs neighbor was now blaring his radio. Finally, my mother wiped her eyes, and I had a sense of foreboding.

> A girl of good family. A pretty girl, reasonably smart with no starry aspirations. Yet somehow she got embroiled with small time producers, shady filmmakers, and the like and then vanished like a loosely threaded sequin blown off a dress. This sort of behavior was unheard of in our family going back seven generations! I think Mahwah convinced her all she would have to do was escort his wealthy young friends to functions, parties, and business affairs. It would make her rich and make him happy. Remembering how his eyes strayed

away from her, Ritu agreed. Still Harini did nothing.

On that final night, Ritu was supposed to be out of town with a friend of Mahwah. At the restaurant, he probably ordered French food and offered to help her with the silverware. Later he probably invited her to his room. I cannot say how she felt at that moment. Or how she reacted. I imagine at nineteen you tend to disregard the consequences.

The ugly truth of her new life must have finally hit her between the eyes, both numbing and heightening the senses. Who knows what she hoped to accomplish, but in that state, she fled and landed unexpectedly on Mahwah's terrace at an evening affair. No one ever found out what transpired there except there was a bit of a row... people heard shouts, cries, and then a hush. The party went on till the early hours.

Ritu was found on her own bed, in her own home by a servant when he went in to clean her room around midday. She was wrapped in a white sheet, her hair spread out like a halo. She was stiff as a board. There were bruises on her back, her neck, and her head. It appeared she was strangled and then thrown off a balcony or other high ground. She was just a girl, Saya, unschooled, drifting with every passion, flung to the earth, and crushed to death. And what was her crime? A premature attempt to flap her wings?

We don't know how she got home. It's possible Mahwah's thugs sneaked in, carrying her as far away from the scene of crime as possible. Do you know at the court hearing not a single witness came forth with the specifics? Only vague statements: *It was too dark, Your Honor ... I was too drunk to notice, Your Honor ... I was not in the immediate area, Your Honor* ... such cowards! Such ghouls! And in the gossip columns, a single hasty sentence, "Unsung ending for unknown starlet!" Can you believe it, one's entire time on this planet summed up with a few buzz words by a callous journalist interested only in being the first to report a story?

My mother's shoulders shook, and I stood up quietly.

"Where are you going dear?"

"To Aunt Harini's, to condole with her."

"But this happened years ago, Saya!"

"I know, but she is still grieving, isn't she? And still feels quite alone." I held my mother's eyes until she lowered her own. ♦

Swamini

For this, my life is worth examining. Is it not?

*- **Geet***

Peacock feathers spread over the centerfold like tapestry. My mother traced her fingers delicately over his crown, awestruck by the colors winking in the canted light and the sheer joy of the creature dancing in the rain. Gently, she closed the old *National Geographic* magazine as if it contained almost too much beauty. "The trouble with paradise," she said reflectively, "is that it lulls you into believing you are there to stay, that you've reached your journey's end."

I waited for her to go on.

"I was thinking of my niece, Deepa's daughter Geet. Over three years, and she still insists she is happy living in an ashram in Mt. Abu," she said, perplexed.

"Is she a nun?" I asked facetiously.

"Swamini, they are called, the female priests."

"Geet, a swamini! What a colorful family we have, Mum. On the one hand, poor, troubled, materialistic Ritu and on the other hand a swamini!"

My mother admonished me with a look. "It is not a joking matter," she said. "Such a pretty girl. Such a happy girl she was. According to my sister, she was a gifted student, voted most likely to succeed. She dressed well, carried her art supplies in a tote bag decorated with pieces of glass, wore beads and baubles like all girls her age; a typical, modern beauty."

My mother was warming up to the story.

> And if you walked down the halls of the Art Institute where she spent four wonderful years, you can see her joyful paintings hanging on the walls and her charcoal drawings in glass fronted cabinets: a collage of food vendors, their carts spilling over with ripe mangoes,

> apples, cherries; lights wrapped around the ocean like a queen's necklace, the water ablaze with multi-colored gems; or a group of naked children plunging into a tub of water drawn from a well. You can almost hear their shrieks of excitement; feel their shivers of joy. I ask you, does that sound like the work of a troubled girl given to pessimism, afflicted with demons, reflecting Buddha-like in the middle of night on the meaning of life?

"Mum, you don't have to be troubled or pessimistic to want to try and understand the meaning of life," I said, somewhat condescendingly.

Absorbed in the story, my mother continued as if she hadn't heard me:

> After art school, Geet had a bit of trouble finding the right job. For every fresh art graduate, Saya, there are hundreds of experienced graphic artists waiting in line. And there being no pressing need, Deepa is a wealthy woman after all, her daughter spent her time painting for pleasure and 'seeing' the boys her parents arranged for her to meet.
>
> On that score, too, the stars did not seem to

align. There was one boy she actually liked. A verbal contract was made, but on the day of the engagement, the boy called her in distress, said he was not attracted to her, and wanted to study abroad. He begged her to call off the engagement and save him from his father's wrath. She did.

Soon after that, she went to Mt. Abu, ostensibly for a holiday, but I am convinced Geet was more hurt and humiliated by this latest rejection than she let on and it was this incident that triggered her need for peace and reflection.

She wrote home often and sounded quite content, so at first, Deepa was not worried. They had made certain she was in a safe place, a dull place even, Deepa privately thought, but gave in to her wish for a few weeks of ashram living. "A little yoga, a little meditation, and simple vegetarian cooking never hurt anybody," her father said in his jovial way, patting his own well-padded belly.

"Besides, Geet has always followed the trends. Remember when she sported a nose ring and when she insisted on a diet of just carrot juice and eggs twice a week? And the time she insisted we treat our servants as equals and let them sit at the table with us?" He laughed, as if the idea was even remotely funny.

Anyway, three months of Mt. Abu was quite enough by anyone's standards. Deepa asked her to come home, and you know, Saya, Geet refused! She claimed she had a job at the Ashram that paid her enough that she could live there and study under the Gurus. What was it that she needed to study there that couldn't be learned under her own roof with the help of private tutors?

Deepa was frantic. One moment she feared the so-called pundits were predators preying on her daughter, and next that she was being inducted into a cult and would resort to animal sacrifices and nightly orgies and whatnot. It was ridiculous! I finally told her to get out her bedroll, pack a few woolen underclothes, and let's go see for ourselves what her daughter was up to. She said Geet had ordered her not to visit. So I asked, "Is Mt. Abu no longer open to tourists? We will stay in a hotel and find a way to meet with her." And that's how we landed on that hilly resort.

Geet looked wonderfully composed and happy in the Ashram. The cool mountain air made her cheeks look like red apples, and the yoga obviously agreed with her physique. I noticed she did not talk in her usual bubbly style – more like a tinkling stream than an erupting wave. But that might simply be the narcotic effect of the surroundings. I mean Saya, in Mt. Abu, there was such amazing stillness. There was only the sound of our footfalls on the matted grass and the rarefied air blowing hither and thither, whispering through bamboo forests, gathering the scent of wild roses and circulating hymns of joy along the surrounding lakes. In the distance, as far as the eye can see, rose the mountains, mighty and dignified as bishops and cutting through the skies, once in a while, a rare bird called you to prayer in those wall-free chambers of God. I envied Geet then and almost wished I could trade places with her. It would be more fitting too, wouldn't it, at this stage of my life?

Deepa begged her to come home. Geet stalled, saying she would consider returning in a few months. At the time, she was in the middle of her studies of the Upanishads and could not break away. In her opinion, it would be wrong, disrespectful to the Gurus.

Before we parted, I tried to divine the real reason she had broken away from family and friends for this remote place, but she simply smiled and said, "Auntie, I want to know who I am. I asked the Guru, and he said, '*Tat Tvam Asi (You Are That).*' I want to understand what *That* is." I have to say, Saya, I was impressed. I wished her luck and told Deepa not to worry.

But the closer I came to the city and home to the laughter of children, the buzzing of commerce, of life teeming with expectation and regeneration, the more my heart sank. Poor girl. So young. So pretty. How will she ever meet a man on those hills?

Geet kept putting off her trip back home. Deepa was, in turn, furious and frantic. By now, her husband too was upset. He flew to Mt. Abu and threatened he would have the place shut down if the Gurus did not release her. They said she was free to go. Always had been. He called the local police and declared she was a runaway who should be placed in his custody. Geet told the police she was 21 years old and an adult. She then took her father aside and said in so many words, she would file a complaint against him that he was an abusive, neglectful father if he did not leave her alone. He wept like a child.

"Do you not care that you are hurting us?" he asked in that tone parents are sometimes forced to use to get their way.

She upbraided him gently. "I worked hard and was a top student. I did not blow your money or drive from disco to disco in skimpy clothes and gin on my breath. I did not smoke marijuana behind the bushes or run with boys. I respected your rules and asked for nothing. Now, all I want is to be left alone to pursue a life of study and reflection and understand the teachings of our Gurus. So tell me, am I hurting you, or are you hurting me?"

It was then he told her she was free. He would

not bother her any more. Was she sorry she made her father weep? She probably was, but she knew she would be sorrier if she did not follow her heart.

Then Deepa played her "mother" card. She had me make a long distance call to the head of the Ashram, suggesting he send her home at once because her mother was seriously ill.

I interrupted, "Did she come?"

"Yes, but just for a few days," Mother said and told me the rest:

Geet was very tender with her mother, even though she knew the illness was feigned, and quietly explained her life was now in Mt. Abu, and in a few years, she was hoping to be appointed as a swamini. Her parents had done their job and could do nothing more for her.

"And what of marriage, of children?" Deepa asked.

"My need for knowledge is greater," she said.

"Why can't you do both? Pursue knowledge and have a family?"

"And do justice to neither?" Geet countered.

"How will you live without friends, family, a husband's love?" Deepa finally asked, wringing her hands.

"With the grace of God," Geet said and went about her chores.

But it wasn't that simple. Deepa still has not given up. She goes to Mt. Abu twice a year and looks in on Geet. In the past, she always returned dejected and beaten, but these days she walks with a lighter step. After her last visit, she confided that she sensed something different in her daughter. "When I said my goodbyes to her, she no longer looked like one who was walking past the societal Pandora's Box into a sanctum of peace, but like one who was lost within its confines and did not know her way out. Her eyes held an admission her lips would not utter.

"I have a feeling she was asking for help." Those were her words.

I asked, "You are willing to travel all that distance with your bad knee and problem heart based on a feeling?"

"Yes," Deepa sighed.

"For how long?"

Deepa said, "She is my daughter, Jaya. For as long as she is lost, I will try and find her."

I was profoundly moved by Aunt Deepa's stubborn refusal to give up her daughter to God or the Ashram or whatever. Before hearing this story, she had not struck me as a woman of tenacity, with her sweet round face and artless chatter.

Impulsively, I turned to my mother. "You'd do the same for me, wouldn't you, if I were lost or had run away to some inaccessible place?"

My mother, as she often did, answered my question with one of her own. "How much do I love you? You must ask your own heart." ◆

The Disposable Lighter

Maybe happiness is a luxury, convention cannot afford.
- Nina

"Do you have any plans today?" my mother asked, placing the tea tray beside me and ruffling my hair.

"Yes. I'm going to become a swamini like Geet." I giggled, yawned, and stretched luxuriously. My mother stopped me with a look. "Just joking, Mum. Hair, shopping, and lunch with Raina. You want to join us?" She looked at me in a pleased sort of way although she shook her head firmly.

"Me? You go out and enjoy yourself. And do buy yourself some nice shoes, and why are your arms so rough?"

I assumed the last was a rhetorical question and buried my nose in my first restorative cup of tea. In the shower I grinned to myself as I tried to exfoliate my rough arms with a plastic brush, half its bristles worn off like teeth from grinding. That's my mum. Quite certain I am close to perfect if only I would stay out of the sun and moisturize.

At 11 a.m., I pressed my hand against the doorbell, letting it chime my arrival. I expected my friend, who is really a second cousin from my mother's side, to open the door. Instead, a pretty girl with a cheery smile and hooped earrings let me in. I sniffed the air and followed her perfume to an inner room where my girlfriend was still fussing over her *kurta*, which seemed a little snug in the middle section.

"What do you think, leave it on or change?"

"Needs a little altering," I said.

"So, change," she decided and thrust the *kurta* over her neck, not at all self-conscious.

"I'll be leaving now," said a voice behind me, making me jump and step on her toes. I hadn't realized my perky little usherette was still in the room.

"Sorry!"

"It's quite okay," she said, but the little stumble made her drop her purse from which spewed a mishmash of lipsticks, perfume, keys, loose change, and a bright yellow, plastic, disposable cigarette lighter onto the floor.

I bent to help her and felt rather than saw her blush as she hastily threw the lighter into her purse and snapped it shut.

"I'm really awfully sorry. I didn't realize..."

"It's no problem at all. I'll be out for the day. Bye. Enjoy yourselves," she said over her shoulder as she whisked herself off.

"Who was that, Raina?" I asked.

"Sister-in-law," she muttered and then turned to her wardrobe to look for another shirt.

"No way!" I'd met her sister-in-law. In fact I'd attended her brother's wedding, a rather sweet but poignant affair where both the bride's and the groom's relatives kept their fingers crossed and breathed a collective sigh when the ceremony was over. The truth was her brother was mentally challenged and the girl, a mousy little thing who kept her head low as if bending under the weight of her decision, suffered from a speech disorder and had not spoken since she was eight years old. Or so I was told. Yet here she was, like one of those people on TV who have had an extreme makeover all polished, perfumed, and out the door.

My girlfriend, however, did not look impressed. In fact, she looked a bit green around the gills and all through lunch stuck to generalities, cleverly steering the conversation away from her family. I got the hint and decided not to bring up her sister-in-law's amazing transformation from mouse to mistress. After lunch, we simply sat companionably side-by-side getting our hair done and indulging in Hollywood gossip.

A side effect of green tea taken in conjunction with a Thai massage in the late afternoon is that it leaves you in that sated and trusting state where you dreamily unlock the secrets of your heart. She began talking, almost to herself, after we'd driven back to her home and locked ourselves in her room like old times.

"Saya," she said, "did you notice the little cigarette lighter fall out of my sister-in-law's purse?"

"Yes, I did actually. It was such a bright yellow. Why?"

"It doesn't belong to my brother," she said. I looked at her curiously.

"Well, I guess it belongs to her then. How come it bothers you? Are you worried that she smokes?"

"She doesn't smoke, Saya. How many Indian housewives do you know that smoke?"

"Then what?"

She stared at me in a pitying sort of way, like one waiting for the light bulb to go on. My mind lurched into action. "Surely you are not suggesting she's having an affair?"

She heaved a sigh of relief that I'd made the intuitive leap at last even as she turned a shade pink. "Yes, it is true. We are all aware of it."

I turned this information in my head, over and over like foreign currency that has somehow strayed into a purse of local coins. "What about your brother? Is he aware too?"

"Not him, of course. How would he know?" Now she glared as if I had overlooked a horrible, self-evident truth.

I placed a hand over hers. Obviously, the tranquilizing effect of the Thai massage was wearing off. She burst into tears. "I'm sorry, Saya."

"No. What is going on? Surely we can fix it?"

She shook her head. "I will tell you what's going on. Promise you won't judge." Puffing her cheeks, she released her pent-up anguish and said softly:

> When Nina stepped into our home, my brother's life found meaning for the first time. Before Nina, he was like a helpless infant holding out his arms, trusting he would be gathered and comforted by the world of adults, unaware that the world saw him only peripherally, like a broken toy on a busy street, and passed him by with a derisive glance. Only my mother tended to him full time. Washing, cooking, doctor's appointments, and feeding Neil, it was all in a day's work for her and occasionally, when it suited, for the rest of us. I guess, as a child, his life was fairly comfortable seeing that we kept him in a bit of a cocoon, but then he sprouted up, his voice changed, his face broke out, he discovered his genitals, and my mother's days went from manageable stress to being buried under an extra large load of humiliations.

It began by his peeking into the neighbor's window, sticking his tongue out at the girls. They complained he was watching them as they dressed. We told him to stop, and he did for a while. Then he began spending hours in the bathroom with my *Cosmo Woman* catalogs, obviously masturbating, and when he wasn't doing that, he watched TV. It would have been sort of funny if it hadn't been so pathetic. He would go close to the screen and pat the girls' hair and make kissing noises.

I asked him once if he knew they were not real, and he said, "Of course, I know, I'm not retarded!" I was shocked he said the word aloud but more shocked he *knew* the word at all and used it in context. It was then that I realized, maybe he was simple, but surely he needed to live up to his full potential, whatever that might be? Here I was, a licensed psychologist who had spent the entire twenty-eight years of her life openly ignoring her sibling's special needs. Something to be ashamed of, wasn't it? So I tried making up for lost time.

I saw to it that Neil learned the difference between private and public behavior. I made him a list of dos and don'ts, very specific ones, Saya, like don't peep, don't touch yourself in public, don't touch strangers, and so on. In time, he learned to behave in an acceptable manner, and he began taking pride in his appearance, obsessively so as a matter of fact. He even began running small errands for us, which he carried out to the letter. He is a good-looking boy with regular features, and from a little distance can easily attract a flirtatious glance or two. When you get closer though, and you notice those shining hazel eyes without the corresponding glimmer of intelligence you realize what a cruel joke the gods have played on our Neil.

In any event, when Neil confided to me he wanted to be married and "make sex" as he put it, I actually began giving it serious thought. I realized the only chance he had was to find a girl who had special needs herself. We learned about Nina through friends. Apparently, she hadn't spoken since the age of eight when she'd suffered some childhood trauma. We broached the subject somewhat tentatively with her parents. They were surprisingly receptive. Nina met my brother, and before any of us had truly grasped the enormity of the situation, they had tied the knot!

"You were at the wedding, remember?"

The thing is they were so happy at first. They behaved more like two kids who had discovered in each other the traits they lacked in themselves, things they could share and had missed sharing with another all their lives. They would sleep and rise together like one body with eight limbs and chase each other, actually playing tag in the house and jumping over furniture. We tolerated it because Neil was happy. Nina made him see himself as a full-fledged person, a purveyor of entertainment, a partner in crime. Imagine how that must have felt to one who, at age twenty-four, was still tucked in bed at 8 p.m. so that the grownups could spend quality time without him. What is so weird is we had never considered his happiness before, as if it were a luxury he couldn't afford. But once he had it, it became all that mattered. We did not want to do anything that would jeopardize this abundance of blessings.

Because Nina never spoke, we initially made the mistake (yes, ours was a family prone to making many mistakes) of assuming her level of intelligence was equivalent to Neil's. Clearly, we were wrong. She watched the news and documentaries with a sort of brooding focus and was constantly running to the library for books. Her taste in reading was eclectic, from Madame Curie to Salinger, from Mary Higgins Clark to Carl Sagan. I was impressed. More than that, I was very curious. Why did a girl like Nina marry Neil? What was the trauma that snatched her voice like a devil snatching away a soul? Was it a physical trauma... was it psychogenic? I had a feeling it was, for she was always scared around everyone but the family. She never left home without a servant chaperoning her and was terrified of the dark to the extent that when we once had a power cut, she thrashed around so maniacally we thought she would hurt herself. I remember lighting so many candles one would think we were about to hold a séance, and I'm not being facetious.

So this is what I did, Saya. I took her to a psychiatrist. I guess her parents didn't consider therapy because a cure is never guaranteed and it is expensive, but mostly, I bet, because of the stigma associated with mental problems. Anyway, she was under my colleague Dr. Segal's care for almost three years, and within the first year itself we began to see changes. She walked straighter, her head held high; she dressed better and attempted walks without the servant. Then about eight months ago she spoke her first word. Nothing dramatic. Neil held one of her books aloft and wouldn't give it to her. I guess he wanted to play.

"Give me," she said.

It was an electric moment, and she looked at me almost puzzled, as if it was I who had spoken, and all of us – Dad, Mother, Neil, and I -- drew closer as if getting ready for a group hug. I whispered, "Say it again!" So she did. As you saw for yourself, she's quite the little canary now. Found her voice at last.

"Oh my God, Raina you must be so proud! It's all your doing you know."

"Yes. Very proud, but lately I feel as though I've created a monster."

"Explain that," I said, puzzled.

"Our family has given her everything she could possibly ask for. We are responsible for the person she is today, and now she treats my brother differently. Where once they played tag and hide and seek, she now buries herself in a book. Where once they ran out for ice cream or candy or some childish thing, now she shrugs him off easily, saying, "I'm busy." In the evening, she insists on helping with the dinner and dishes, then does a load of wash, and irons a few dozen shirts. I used to think, "My, she really is a busy little beaver, what a great help to Mother," but I discovered she was procrastinating; looking for ways to delay going to their bed. By the time she's done with her chores, he's asleep, or she's too tired and has a headache, body ache, you know what I mean. This I figured out because I've seen the way she looks at him when he stares in the same exact way at a stark wall, a phantasmagoric sunset, or a new born baby -- his eyes without commentary, reflecting only the emptiness that extends from one corner of his mind to the other -- and I swear I see a deep-seated contempt. How I wish she would also see the way he sometimes look at her, Saya. She is his sun, his moon, his Venus, and all the stuff of fantasy in between. How can she miss seeing that?

A couple of months ago, our regular laundry man fell sick and sent us our laundry via his daughter. It was through her that I first had an inkling something was up.

To my sister-in-law she said, "Oh, you are here! But I thought you lived in Skyward building."

I marched up to her and asked rather sharply, "Why would you think that?"

"She often answers the door when I go there," the delivery girl said, now all wide-eyed and probably relishing the thought of the furor she knew she was about to create.

"You are mistaking me for someone else, you

idiot," my sister-in-law interjected and shut the door on the girl. But guilt sat on her face like a mole and she avoided eye contact for the rest of the day.

Before the rumor mill began churning out dirt in earnest, Saya, I made a conscious decision to get to the bottom of things and began following Nina about like a sleuth in flat slippers. In just a few days, I learned that she was indeed seeing someone, a divorced attorney who lives barely a mile away in Skyward building. I confronted her, and she admitted it readily. My heart ached for my childlike brother, for what she had done to him and for what she was about to do, judging from her comment, "I'm glad you've found out. I've been waiting for the right moment to talk to you about it."

It seems they met at the local bakery. Nina was coming out of the store with a paper sack full of sweet rolls when she bumped into him. She dropped her sack and the baked goods spilled out, sending a couple of them spinning down the street.

"Oh dear, your buns are rolling out of control,"

said the man.

The hilarity of this remark struck them both at the same time, and they began laughing till the tears streamed down their cheeks. He helped her collect the stuff and said in passing, "You should buy these at exactly 7 p.m. every night. That's when they come out of the oven." She waved her thanks and went on home that evening, but the next day, decided to check for herself. She joined a line of people snaking outside the store, and at 7 p.m. the baker pulled the tray out of the oven with a forked rod, filling the shop with the heavenly, comforting goodness of raisin bread. Suddenly hungry, she ordered a few rolls, and as she dug in her purse for cash, she felt a hand on her shoulder.

"So when do you plan on eating those?" It was the jokester from the day before.

"For breakfast, I guess," she smiled

"You should have one right now when it's bursting with freshness, in the corner café where you get the best coffee in the country."

She rolled her eyes. "I'm not going to the café

by myself."

"No. You are going with me."

And that, according to Nina, is how they went out on their first date. Things progressed very quickly, and Nina, a married woman from a solid middle class background of fine, upstanding parents, found herself in the throes of an affair that she had no intention of breaking off. I asked if she felt no guilt, no shame for ignoring her marital vows. She said that what Neil didn't understand wouldn't hurt him, and the bitch just went right on with her lying, cheating ways. Can you believe that, Saya? A few weeks later I told her she was wrong if she thought Neil didn't know anything. He was miserable. He paced about the balcony for hours after she went out, and his face lit up like a candle when she returned. He wasn't eating or sleeping or laughing as before. I reminded her that his being inarticulate did not mean he was clueless. He was very intuitive. She, of all people, ought to know that.

She replied, so heartlessly it took my breath

away, "Perhaps he feels a little excluded, but he was born clueless. We all know that."

I told her about the rumors riding on the shoulders of laundrymen and janitors and neighborhood gossips and how my family did not deserve this. She merely shrugged and averted her eyes. I was so upset I wanted to get into Dr. Segal's files and dig into her past. I thought if I could unearth some family skeleton I might be able to use it as leverage. Of course, I didn't go through with that Saya. I'm not a monster, and Dr. Segal wasn't going to break any confidentiality laws.

Desperate, all I could come up with to say to her was, "The fact that you are even going out and about with that smile on your face and that lilt in your voice is because of me, and this is how you repay my kindness?"

I'll never forget her voice, so heavily laced with bitterness. "I am grateful to you, and I repay you every day of my life by staying tied to my *child groom.*"

"You liked him well enough when you first got married," I said.

She retorted, "I was living a lie. Use your imagination, Raina. Think about how it is for me. All I want is what all women should have, the right to an ordinary day, a conversation with an adult, an evening in a restaurant simply talking about mundane things, the weather, cricket, the new book by Rushdie. Instead I sit at home, wiping his chin with a kerchief and playing hide and seek. When he makes love to me, I feel like a wooden doll, not a woman with needs of my own."

I was finally stumped, Saya. I didn't know whether to hate her or pity her, and I realized no amount of emotional blackmail would make her love my brother. I told my parents everything at a family meeting. I suggested we should ask her to divorce Neil.

Raina turned her face to the wall. She seemed spent. I longed to know the outcome but hung back. I wanted to be supportive without being overly curious. After all, she was sharing a very personal story.

"My parents don't want them to divorce," she said finally. "They spoke to Nina. They actually told her they quite understood she had outgrown their son, and who could blame her for that, but she was after all a married woman so perhaps a compromise was in order. She could go about her life consorting with another man as long as she stayed under our roof as Neil's wife. Nina was fine with it. It seems they are *all* fine with it. Ours is a very progressive family." Raina's mouth twisted in anguish.

My eyes fairly popped, "But does she not want to leave? What's preventing her?"

"So far, her new beau is perfectly happy with the status quo and has not really offered to marry her. I expect he wants to have his cake and eat it too," she muttered. "I should have let him be, let my brother live out his childlike life lost in daydreams on a footstool by the television, untouched by these feelings of distrust and betrayal that torture him so. I made him believe he could be normal, be happy, and look where my meddling has left him, where it has left all of us."

I looked at my friend and marveled at her big, generous heart that she did not know she possessed. "You can't protect anyone forever, Raina, including your brother. You gave not *one* but *two* people a chance to live a fuller life, driven by hope. In your heart, you have to know that is the truth and they are better off for the experience."

She looked unconvinced.

"What you did for her was wonderfully unselfish. You gave Nina her voice back." I said emphatically. "And who knows what turn your brother's life might take next. You don't happen to have a crystal ball, do you?" I chucked her under her chin and left the matter at that.

On my way out, I spied the colorful Nina, a small smile playing on her rosy lips and thought again of the little yellow lighter in her purse, a disposable keepsake she could ignite with the flick of a thumb and dispel the darkness as her husband lay snoring by her side. I shook off the image and hailed a cab.

The night spread before me like my favorite blanket, soft from washing, woven with the familiar smells of sunlight and soap, powder and lotion. There was a chill in the air. Mum had suggested I carry a shawl before I left. Of course, I did not listen. My eyes welled up, I have no idea why. Perhaps I simply needed a nap. But not before I had a steaming cup of comfort à la mama and her good old-fashioned predictability. I yawned and urged the cabbie to hurry. ♦

The Swallower of Secrets

"What lies beyond this dry well?" asked the crab.

"Loneliness," said his mother.

"A trap," said his brother.

"Death," said his father.

The crab looked first this way, then that.

"In that case, what's the difference?" He said and inched his way out of the well.

- Singh

I tossed and turned in bed unable to find my sweet spot and curl into it for the night. When I slept at last, people I hadn't seen in years as well as those I visited the day before – Raina, Neil, his bold wife and her cigarette lighter, and curiously, an old family servant called Singh entered my dreams and I was not quite gracious, wishing them gone. When at long last I heard the clang of milk cans against a rusty bicycle frame, I breathed a sigh of relief. The milkman must be making his rounds. My mother would soon be up.

"You didn't get a good night's rest," Mum said as she handed me the bed tea. I nodded gloomily.

"I was dreaming about Singh of all people. Mum, whatever happened to him? I didn't see him at Aunt Dina's this time."

Mum didn't answer immediately, so, of course, I knew she was trying to figure out how best to give me bad news.

"What? Is he dead?"

She flinched. "Don't say such things Saya. Only good thoughts at the sacred hour, remember? To answer your question, no, he is not *gone*. He has retired. He lives with his family back in Nepal."

Retired. Family. Nepal. The words shot out of her mouth

like bullets, spattering my forehead with exclamation points.

"Do servants actually retire? I thought Aunt Dina was his family! He left Nepal when he was seventeen and must be now going on eighty! Is anyone even there?"

Mother frowned in amusement. "So many questions so early in the day."

I pursed my lips motioning her to please go on, and she propped two pillows against the wall to get comfortable in a semi-upright position. I put a sheet over her legs. She pushed it back, covering only her feet. My mum's feet were always cold. Finally, she began:

> Your Aunt Dina was only recently married when her husband realized she knew very little about the running of the house other than ordering about servants, so being a good, kind man, he got Singh to manage things. They did not get along at first, you know. Singh was a year older than your aunt, and they were both about the same height. Originally Singh came to your uncle looking to do odd jobs at his store. He was told there was no opening there, but if he could lend a hand to his young bride, he would be paid well. He agreed, probably out of

desperation and the fact that he would be getting free room and board.

They fought like brother and sister over control of the kitchen. I remember coming upon them once. He held one end of a squash while she tugged at the other end, not sure what they planned to do with it as neither of them could cook. Anyway, I remember grabbing the squash out of their hands before they did any damage. They watched me like children as I chopped and sautéed it with onions, tomatoes and a half-inch piece of ginger. Singh was always respectful toward me you know, even though I was younger.

I couldn't help interrupting. "That's because you look so dignified and efficient," I said.

Mum never did learn to say thank you; it was not her way. She simply acknowledged the compliment with her customary nod and small tilt of the mouth before picking up the story:

Your aunt had all three children, including two miscarriages, within the first six years of marriage. Before children, you can play the child yourself, Saya, demanding ice cream, perfume, silks, and entertainment. Children bring with them a shifting and a softening. Brimming with nourishment, a mother is moved to nurture, wanting only to be left alone that she may soothe and sate the infant sucking on her breast. His mouth is the only caress she needs, his gurgling and cooing the only theatre she enjoys. His demands supersede the demands of husband, society, and friends.

Your uncle, perplexed at first that his wife seemed forever tired and keeping the same hours as the little ones, soon resigned himself to longer hours at the shop, giving Singh increased responsibility and a hefty raise for all round assistance but mostly for his guard-dog like vigilance around the children. For vigilant he was, to the point that the other servants sulked and complained that he was domineering and behaved as if he was not one of them.

He wouldn't let the maids touch the children unless they washed their hands with soap first; he stood over their heads as they boiled the milk and filled the baby bottles, demanding they test a drop on their wrists before they handed the bottle to Dina; he shushed them and told them they couldn't listen to the radio in the house because it was a bad influence on growing children. But their worst complaint was that he treated them like potential thieves and hovered close to the rice and grain bins, contending they were stealing some of it away in the folds of their *kurta*s when they left for the day.

You know it is not certain even if they ever did steal. Mind you, a little stealing is acceptable. It's human nature, like taking shampoo and washcloths from hotels just because they are there. Of course, housemaids probably did it to feed those extra mouths that keep popping open. My point is, soon it was impossible to get a servant to work for them, with Singh sniffing around. He became the President of the household, with your uncle as Prime Minister and your aunt, Queen Victoria. A sort of family of important people with no direct reports.

Mum giggled like a child who was amused at her own joke, then settled and continued:

When Singh was around twenty-one, he had saved enough cash to take his first trip home. Also, by now he was the glue that held the household together and felt confident that in his absence, no maid could threaten his position with her politicking ways. He was a clever young man who knew he must not get careless and must continue to bring more to the table to secure a permanent place in their lives. Already, your uncle trusted him implicitly with the children. And, being a man, your aunt had no qualms about letting him do the heavy lifting around the house. Trudging blithely up a nine-foot ladder, he cleared the cobwebs off fans, ceiling lights, and the corner of walls. He hauled down the drapes and took them to the terrace where he beat the dust out and let them air out in the sun. He poked and pried behind the kitchen sink and the refrigerator and teetered on the window ledge, scouring ants, bird droppings, and whatnot.

And after he saw your aunt weep at some snide comment from neighbors and friends about her cooking, he astutely watched my every move in the kitchen when I went down to visit, and within six months he became a wonderful cook. Better than me, in fact, for he could generously use cashews and cream and spices too expensive for my purse. At long last, after he overheard Aunt Dina on the phone admit she was completely dependent on Singh and could not imagine running a household without his agility, his common sense, and his problem solving skills, he decided he could take a chance and go on a holiday.

He was gone two months, leaving your aunt so bewildered and overwrought that your uncle had to ask each of us sisters to help out. He returned a dreamy-eyed young man, given to humming and definitely more tractable. When pushed, Singh finally admitted he had been married while on his visit, and that his bride was to live with his parents until he could afford to bring her to the city. To this day, no one has met a member of his family.

The children were fast growing up. Singh's duties now included preparing and bringing them their lunch tiffins to school, washing and ironing their uniforms and generally nagging them and your aunt to death. I often thought of him as a woman trapped in a boy's body, itching and chafing to get out.

The only time Singh was cowed a little was when your aunt threatened she would go away for a month to her father's home, if uncle did not have a talk with Singh about his high-handed ways. Then for a few days, he sulked and behaved and showed his displeasure by hiding a uniform badge or an important schoolbook, and leaving Dina's favorite blouse to fade in the sun so that she would call each of us, wringing her hands, for advice. What could we say, Saya, except he was a gem and a prize, and where can you get such wonderful servants these days who made mouthwatering dishes *and* allowed her to attend bridge parties, confident the kids were safe at home doing their homework? So she had to grin and bear it, and in fact, over the years, not only she but the rest of us also forgot his status and regarded him as a member of the family.

My mother paused and levered her hands to raise herself from the bed. "We will have breakfast first," she said, "Before I tell you the rest," and trudged off to the kitchen not giving me a chance to protest.

Over toast, eggs, tea, and more tea, I asked, "But all of Aunt Dina's kids loved Singh, did they not even though he was a bit of a curmudgeon?"

"Of course! And why would they not? What is the one thing most in the world that three hormonal young pups want? A lock on their secrets, that's what. And Singh was a true swallower of secrets."

"Oooh, secrets! Do tell," I encouraged her. Smiling, she continued:

> Dina's oldest son went through a couple of rebellious years. Many a time, he now tells us with a laugh, he came home, his shirt torn off at the shoulder, his body scratched and torn from fighting with the local boys. Singh kept watch from the terrace, and as soon as he spied the boy, he ran around the back with fresh clothes and bandages, disguising the damage enough so as not to alarm the family. Later, he began running across to meet the boys on a daily basis – Dina thought he was getting soft in his old age – but it was more so he could sniff out the cigarettes or liquor on their breath. This he

handled with admonitions, chewing gum, licorice candy, and other breath fresheners.

You might say this was misguided loyalty, but although the boys did not understand it at the time, it bought him their trust *and their obedience*. You see, in Singh's eyes, there were two commandments carved in stone. One, you will excel in school, which they did, partly because they were smart children but partly too because if they ever slackened in their studies, Singh had only to warn them with a look: I know your secrets, shape up or else. And two, you will not deflower a girl before you are married. He had no commandment for Dina's daughter. Singh always treated Simi as a precious, perfect little gem who did not have to be told how to conduct herself.

Where he got his ideas, I do not know. Perhaps he understood intuitively the family values Dina and your uncle tried to instill in their children and adopted them very early on, as his own. Or perhaps it was just his nature.

Suddenly Mum giggled so hard, she had a coughing fit. I did not understand what was funny.

I told you your older cousin went through some rough years. As he got older, girls were naturally a big part of his life. He went out to parties and discotheques every night. Well, one time Singh spotted his car parked on a side street in the dead of night. Naturally, he was not alone. You know what he was up to, so I won't paint a picture, Saya.

Would you believe it, Singh went to every fancy looking car on the street and tried forcing the door open just to make the alarm go off. Imagine flashing lights and shrieking alarms suddenly going off on the entire street! The racket was so great your cousin sped off with his shirt unbuttoned and lipstick on his collar afraid the police were after him!

Then there was Dina's younger boy who fell in love with a Muslim girl. Of course, this was not just monkey business it was a serious, life and death situation. Singh knew he had to treat it delicately. If he confronted the boy, he would only deny the affair and find ways to elude Singh, so Singh sent a note to the girl's father asking him to safeguard his daughter's virginity. He said in the note that if the boy she was fooling around with came to any harm, he would personally spread rumors around the city that she was no longer "pure." The affair ended that day.

"Oh my God! Did he have to do that? They may have truly been in love," I said, aghast.

"Be sensible, Saya," Mother said. "If either the Hindu or the Muslim fundamentalists found out, one of the kids would surely have been murdered. Those were bad days."

"I think Singh was just frustrated, he didn't have a girl," I said petulantly. "What about his wife? Did he ever visit her again or bring her over to visit?"

Mum explained, "Barely nine months after their wedding, she gave birth to twins. By the time he saw her again, they were bare bottomed little runts running around the village unrecognizable from the local farm creatures. He was acutely pained, I think, used as he was to seeing Dina's kids starched and powdered for school or play. He doubled the amount he was sending home and strongly advised his wife to put them in school. He saw them only one more time, years later. They were eking out a living for themselves and did not acknowledge him as their father. His wife, according to gossip around the neighborhood cigarette shop, was living in sin with another man. Think of Singh, Saya, sending his hard earned money home year after year to this dubious trio. He decided he would not see them again, although he continued to send her money."

We were both silent for a while. It seemed to me there was no right or wrong in the scenario, only a sad sort of pointlessness.

"Wasn't he away for a few years with Aunt Dina's daughter?" I asked after a bit.

"Yes. When your cousin got married and moved out of state, Singh was sent with her to sort of help her settle down just as he'd eased Dina into married life when she was a young bride."

"Was he part of the dowry?" I sniggered.

My mother did not dignify that with a response, but went on:

> He was there to help Simi, and in fact, had it not been for Singh, Dina would never have known

of the privations your poor cousin suffered in her new marital home. A series of bad investments and corrupt partners led to some terrible times for your cousin. Creditors were banging on her door, marching off with her refrigerator, her TV, whatever they could lay their hands on while her husband looked on in his fogged way, and the rest of his family slinked off abroad leaving her, a child reared on pistachios and satin bedspreads, to wring her hands and soak the sheets and look for employment in wretched hole in the wall book shops and clothing stores.

Whenever he saw her in her room, holding her head in her hands, Singh would place before her a steaming glass of hot sugared milk and stay until she drank every drop. He would darken the room and shut the door, letting her rest. When he realized her troubles could not be soothed with milk, it was Singh - a man who feared speaking into the telephone so much he actually thought it harbored evil spirits - who placed the call to your aunt, ordering her to come down and save her daughter from a life of decrepitude. Dina went down at once, of course, and putting aside all the biases we are raised with, cried and embraced him openly and declared him her brother and best friend.

Singh became a sort of hotline for your cousin and perhaps a lifeline for me as well. For as you know, Saya, we faced many storms of our own, so much so that I could no longer afford the short trips to my sisters' homes or the movies or any small outing to cheer myself up. Pride forces us to seal our lips, but love opens its arms and breaks down all resistance. Dina's intuition always kicked in just as I found the walls closing in on me, and she would send Singh with letters of comfort and pouches of aid to squelch my despair. When he graced our door, Saya, I did not see a little servant boy from Nepal, I saw an angel. I insisted he sit on the sofa like the rest of us and plied him with tea and fritters. And so he sat, holding his cup with a delicate air, thin legs dangling abashedly, accustomed as he was to sitting on the floor on his haunches and pouring tea in his saucer and slurping noisily as a mare.

Singh united me with my sister, even if only in

> my mind, and I went back to those few years of my life when I was a carefree child with my *didi*, my sis, bearing the brunt of our stepmother's envy and father's stern gaze. Dina put her own body in front of mine then, and she put her body in front of me again with her comforting letters and emergency funds. Singh knew exactly what she was doing and never said a tactless thing and treated me with even more respect than before.

"There was some trouble with the son-in-law though...?" I fished.

My mother's eyebrows shot skyward before she continued:

> I did not know you'd heard about that. Yes. Well, by now all the kids were adults. When the boys drifted off to their own flats, Aunt Dina invited her daughter and son-in-law to come live with her until they could get their feet on the ground. It was too heartbreaking for her to enjoy her husband's prosperity when her own daughter was chewing her nails over the ever looming end-of-the-month crisis.
>
> Now, I don't know how much of this is true, but

rumor has it, returning from an errand earlier than anticipated, Singh caught the son-in-law in a compromising position with a maidservant. At the time, mother and daughter were out at a girls' luncheon. Apparently he dragged the servant girl by her hair and threw her out of the house, still in a state of undress, and then did a truly astonishing thing. He slapped the man's face hard enough that it left an imprint harsher than any declaration of contempt. He then took Dina aside to keep her daughter's heart intact and told her about the events of the afternoon.

Inexplicably, Saya, Dina was as angry with Singh as she was with her son-in-law. She said no matter how serious the offense, he had no authority to take matters in his own hand and his impertinence had just cost him his job.

Singh looked at your uncle. Your uncle looked at Dina, rooted in indignation, and he told her to do as she saw fit. It was the first time in his life that Singh had to grovel his way back, protesting he got carried away only because he could not bear the thought of seeing your cousin's pain if she ever found out. He worried about Simi as if she was his own child. Finally, Dina relented and let him stay. I think that was the day he understood he was not omnipotent. It was after this incident that Dina too really came into herself. She recognized her own power, and for the first time, there was a hierarchy in the household, with her as "high command."

"And the son-in-law?"

Mum swatted the air, her characteristic response to matters concerning useless, undeserving, men.

I mulled over the Singh story and finally found the contradiction scratching at my brain.

"Wait a minute. You said right at the beginning Singh has retired and lives with his family in Nepal, but later you said, he decided he would *not* ever go back because of his wife's infidelity ..."

The silence was so heavy and went on for such a long time I wondered if my mother had dozed off with her eyes open. One of her sisters did that, and it was very unnerving. But she must have simply been thinking back in time, and went on:

After your uncle passed away, Dina was emotionally and physically quite exhausted. The illness was a big drain on the family coffers, with the extended family and all, they were now three generations under the same roof, each champing at the bit for space, privacy, what have you. Then Singh fell ill and no one seemed to have time for him. He was the family caretaker. No one thought to take care of *him*. Finally, Simi took him to the doctor. They found that he had Alzheimer's.

Aunt Dina was too old to care for him. Neither did she have the means to put him in a place, a nursing home where he would be cared for. They let him stay with them, as he was, for a while, but then he got worse. Once, he went missing and search parties had to go out to find him. He was found by the railway tracks five miles from home. He began using the street as a public latrine, he began stripping in public, he…well, you can imagine.

So he was sent home to Nepal with Dina's grandson chaperoning the trip. Singh's wife and children refused to keep him, so Dina paid to have a hut built close to them so he could stay there. She sends him blankets and sweaters each winter, for he is always cold. Occasionally, he calls from one of those public phone centers still functioning in small villages where cell phones are not yet the fad. Always the same refrain – he is lost and needs to come home. Strange isn't it, that he still remembers the phone number? One can only pray that his family will watch over him out of compassion if nothing else.

My mother fell silent, her index finger teasing the dead skin on her thumb.

"But that's not fair," I blubbered. "What if it was Aunt Dina or Uncle who had Alzheimer's, would they not...?"

"But it wasn't them. It was Singh. Be practical, Saya," Mum said. "What does it matter where he now resides? He is a stranger on any soil."

The phone rang just then, and my mother always fearful of unexpected calls went to answer it with a perplexed look on her face. "It's Sheila," she mouthed. Ah! The aunt who lived abroad for a while and hated it there, I remembered. She will probably keep my mother occupied for the next couple of hours. My heart still heavy, I rose and prepared to get dressed. ♦

Traditional Music

One moment of transcendence – all the rest is failed attempt.
- Rohan

"So Aunt Sheila is still married to that awful man?" I asked my mother when she got off the phone with her sister.

Ever the adult role model, Mum repressed a chuckle and pulled out her look of mild disapproval. "Of course, they have a <u>child</u>, Saya!"

"So, for better or for worse, huh?"

My mother was not familiar with the Roman Catholic vows and thought my statement profound. She nodded thoughtfully. "Yes, for better or for worse, they are man and wife and although we have often wished things could be different, they probably will not ever be." She shut her eyes and I sighed happily. I could feel a story coming. And sure enough, Mum began:

> In the old days, parents had to really scour the field for eligible boys. To marry within the family was considered not only an odious thing, but long before science proved them right the elders truly believed incest resulted in congenital disorders, reduced fertility and mental disabilities. And by "within the family" I mean the family tree, Saya, not just a single unit. So you can imagine how hard it must have been for your grandfather. With thirteen children from two wives and four brothers each with large families of their own, a stream of visitors – uncles, cousins, nephews, and nieces -- poured in from all directions and converged in our abode. Indeed, our home was like a warm embrace for innumerable guests.

Everyone was fed well and treated graciously, but, and this cannot be stressed enough, only as long as they followed the universal code of conduct: harbor only platonic, brotherly feelings for the women and maintain a respectful distance. To abuse the code meant instant eviction. Special servants, with the sole purpose of spying on the younger generation were hired, so you can imagine how softly we'd tread on the floorboards.

By the time your Aunt Sheila was twenty, things were different to the extent that most of us sisters were married and living our separate lives. So there were fewer eyes following Sheila about, ostensibly for her own good. Veena, the youngest, was the only other sibling at home until she married Mahaan. Of course, the odd visitor or two still came knocking, for a job in the city, for a semester in some college, or to help out with the business.

It was in her final year in college when Rohan came to visit. He was a sweet boy, extremely solicitous, soft spoken, and polite, a bit of an introvert as young men from small towns tend to be, always a fat engineering book or novel in his hand. I seem to recall he had small effeminate hands, pink lips, and large intelligent eyes that constantly looked into the distance as if seeking an answer to some impenetrable problem. His hair was dark and curly, his forehead branded with lines and a visibly receding hairline, further conveying the impression of a perplexed young man innocent of the ways of the world. Sheila, on the other hand, was a buxom girl with a sharp silhouette and beautiful almond-shaped eyes that shone, if not with intelligence, with a love for life and all that it had to offer.

Sheila and Rohan started out as cousins mindful of each other's role. He was both older and a man, so it was quite within his rights to ask her to make him a cup of tea if she would be so kind or if she knew who had the morning newspaper or how did she fare in her literature test and did she need any assistance? She did as he asked as a matter of course. All the girls in my parents' home were quite dutiful, as you may have gathered.

Heading home one afternoon from class, she came across Rohan. Apparently, he had a meeting on the same side of town, which was inexplicably cancelled, and someone forgot to notify him. Disgruntled and with a slight headache, he tried to think whether he ought to go back to his office or simply call it a day, when he spied Sheila navigating her way around piles of garbage at the same time trying to ignore a couple of ruffians whistling and smirking and generally making her uncomfortable. She held a couple of books like a shield against her straining breasts in an effort to curtail the twin causes of disturbance. Rohan greeted her and began walking alongside, so that the drifters backed off amicably and crossed the street to harass some other young things instead. By the time the cousins reached home, her books in his willing arms, something, not overtly dramatic occurred. Perhaps a cool breeze mussed her hair pushing a curl out to caress her cheek or her scarf ballooned up to hide her face so that Rohan had to part it aside, and in so doing, felt the delicate translucence of her beaded skin. Just a slight, barely perceptible atmospheric shift, in other words, so that in the time it took for the two to walk home, they could no longer look at each other without blushing.

This I know because it was I who found them playing hide and seek with their eyes as I stood at the front entrance of the house, waiting for a bus. I had spent the afternoon holding my sister-in-law's hands during an asthmatic attack and was on my way home. Sheila, in her nervousness, kept up a steady stream of chatter, taking great pains to let me know their meeting outside the home was coincidental and a good thing too because she was being teased by some boys and on and on. I merely patted her shoulder and suggested that Rohan hail me a cab. He hastened to fulfill my request, relieved to get away from the situation.

On the way home in the bus – yes I got off the cab half way, it was just too expensive – I mulled over the little scene and wondered if it was possible to nip in the bud what could surely become a *Heer Ranjha* situation, you know, star-crossed lovers and all that, but

> decided instead to watch and wait. I had my own set of troubles waiting for me to tackle after all, if you know what I mean.

I shrugged impassively. I did know what she meant, but I could not change my messy past, and gestured her to move on.

> I quite forgot about those two for a few weeks, embroiled as I was in trying to raise money to run the household and manage my health issues. You are old enough to know this, so I don't mind telling you, Saya, menopause is like a visitor from hell whose only intent is to disable you with cold sweats, migraines, and unwarranted depression, and then when you are truly down, reach across and wring the neck of your psyche. With very little insight into this problem since we did not discuss women's issues so frankly in my day, I know I was a suicidal maniac for a while.
>
> Anyway, eventually, I found out that your grandmother and the entire family, except us, naturally, had been invited to a wedding out of town. Not receiving an invitation came as no shock to me. Perhaps my father's cousin

> thought it was kinder not to invite us. A wedding is a huge undertaking and expectations run high. Did we have the means to travel? Could we afford the mandatory silk and nylon attire for the entire family? Could we come up with an envelope with five crisp notes at the very least to nestle in the cushioned satin gift box along with the others? No, to all three, so it was just as well. But that is of no matter now.

My mother pursed her lips and slowly massaged her forehead.

> As I was saying, they were all leaving for this wedding when Sheila begged to be excused saying she had prelims that very week and would lose a year if she did not appear for the exams. Rohan would not go along either, for his employer did not give him the time off, so your grandmother, for once, was at her wits' end. To leave Sheila alone in Rohan's care was unseemly. He had given her no cause for suspicion, but he was a young man and she a young woman. They should not be alone in that three-tiered house with its groping hallways,

endless rooms with canopied beds musty from lack of use, perfect hideaways for lusty hearts, vulnerable minds, and male servants mucking about.

So she reached out to me and convinced me in that devious way of hers to go stay with Sheila and bring along the rest of you for the duration – as if I would leave you behind. Wouldn't that be a nice change, she said. I would have free access to her kitchen and storage bins. I remember thinking one's stomach cannot contain more than it is meant to, whether the storage bins are full or not.

I looked at my mother's face, so unpretentious, so stoic. I marveled at her sensitivity and her intelligence, her determination not to let the residual anguish win the day. Acutely aware of every hurtful moment, every painful exchange, every blow of experience, she undid the knots of pain, restored her equanimity, and gave her elders the respect they certainly did *not* deserve only because it was, for her, the right thing to do.

"I think Grandmother knew, deep down, that you alone could be trusted with the responsibility of running the household in her absence," I said.

"More's the pity," my mother nodded and smiled her soft smile before she continued:

> So we stayed with Sheila while the family was away, and it was not so bad. I was actually a little bored because after years of being my own cleaning woman, chef, and assistant, I did not have enough to do, except order the servants. I turned my mind to other things, like picking fresh flowers and knitting them into garlands for the innumerable portraits of those no longer amongst us, decorating the walls and occasionally strumming on the sitar I found gagged and bound in an attic, its music weeping soundlessly for release.
>
> I did not see much of Rohan except when he was leaving or returning from work with his plain black briefcase that he put quietly by the door every night so he wouldn't forget to take it with him, I assume. I found out what his favorite dishes were and saw to it that they were prepared, simple things like lentils and squash and mango pickle, and I think he was touched. Grandmother gave orders directly to the cook to make plentiful amounts of

whatever was fresh and easily available, but it never occurred to her to find out if the family had any preferences. It was a house, she would say grimly, not a hotel where one could order in. Ironically, Rohan said to me that after I came to help out, it was the first time he felt at home.

One afternoon, I decided to pull down the drapes from every single window and have them freshly laundered. I reached the top floor of the house and heard whispered sounds from within one bedroom. I thought it odd. Servants were not supposed to lurk and whisper, and Sheila and Rohan should have left for college and work respectively. Softly, I pushed the door open.

They were there, those two. Sheila, in nothing but a half-slip, her naked breasts a flagrant blow to the traditional values she had been raised with and Rohan with a dazed expression in his eyes, his legs wrapped around every inch of her body so that you could not tell where one began and the other ended, his arms and chest hirsute like a pubescent ape with black sprigs here and there. Of course, they were as startled

as I was, and as they jumped up, I too jumped
back and ran down the stairs two at a time as if
I were the culprit.

My mother paused to ask for a glass of water and sipped it slowly, trying to recover her poise. I thought it funny how, years later, she could still get flustered at the thought of two people making out, but I dared not giggle as she began again:

> It was dinnertime and still they did not come to the main floor. I knew of course that it was fear and embarrassment that kept them upstairs, but I was annoyed nevertheless. Your uncle had fitted a contraption to the telephone that allowed you to connect with each room, like a makeshift intercom. I called them and said dinner was on the table. Finally, they showed their faces. We ate hurriedly, keeping our heads down. It was easier for me as I could focus on serving you kids and your father, who was listening to a desultory bit of news on the transistor radio and noticed nothing.
>
> Later that evening as I sat sewing in a back room, I heard a knock. It was Rohan with Sheila reluctantly in tow.

"Jaya *didi*," he took my hand. "I'm sorry for our behavior, but you see, I love her and want to marry her as soon as possible." I looked at the effeminate little man, as white as a sheet, and felt a twinge of sorrow and pity. Surely God could have given him broader shoulders! The boy shook where there was no wind and still hoped to ride out the storm.

"You cannot marry Sheila, and you know it, Rohan. Why don't we all forget this has happened? I promise I will tell no one if you promise to stay away from each other. It is an infatuation that may well pass." Sheila, I thought, actually looked a little relieved.

"It will not pass didi," he said. The conviction in his voice sent a tremor down my legs. The tip of his nose and ears were fiery red. His eyes were pink and wet. I thought of a rabbit drowning in rainwater.

"I cannot live without her. If I cannot marry Sheila, I might die."

I wanted to say something glib then, like "Do you think you are enacting a scene out of a Bollywood movie? Snap out of it!" But I couldn't. He was sincere and wretched and his chances abysmal. More than that, his words, coupled with the sight of him, filled me with a sense of foreboding.

"You once took me to a movie, Saya, about two people lost in the desert and how the vultures arced overhead, tracing figures of doom in the skies as the lovers quenched their parched throats with each other's tears. Remember?"

There was little I could do. I hoped to distract myself from these misgivings and said with frankness, "Sheila will not be allowed to marry you, Rohan. I hope it does not come to your ... demise." I turned to my sewing indicating they should leave. They slinked out, leaving a mournful silence in their wake.

It was futile to hope that things would change. I caught them twice more in a compromising position, even after my severe reprimand. When the wedding revelers returned two weeks later, I had no choice but to let your grandmother know. She looked at me the way she used to when I first had the pox, as if it was my fault, like I was a contagion infecting everything I touched. Then she knocked on her husband's door and disappeared inside. A few minutes later, to her angry surprise, I let myself in as well. Never before had I approached my father without appointment. He was behind his desk, his walking stick by his side like a penal instrument, a look of thunder in his eyes. Timorously, I broached the subject of my little sister and her true feelings for Rohan, a good, intelligent boy, and the possibility that he could somehow bring their union to fruition. When I was done, he inclined his head asking me to leave.

"Two weeks later, what do you suppose happened? Sheila found herself engaged not to Rohan but to that tyrant of a man she's still married to today."

"How did they take it? The lovers?"

"You know, I did not really see Rohan after the news broke out. I do know that he moved out of the house and into a paying guest facility on the other side of town," Mother explained.

Sheila seemed quite dry-eyed when I saw her after the news had been broken. She married within the year, so I imagine the activity of being dragged from jeweler to jeweler and merchant to merchant for clothes, lingerie, ornaments, and so on may have aided her recovery. What young girl, especially one as beautiful as Sheila, can resist the attention, the pomp, the sheer extravagance of an Indian wedding? The heady feeling of being the center of the universe made Rohan's pale face disappear like a page torn off at the end of a calendar month.

Oh, it is possible, at the end of the day and alone in her canopied bed, he surfaced in her dreams so that she woke up crying. Possible too that she touched her face every now and then and felt an indefinable ache where his impression lingered like hot breath. And entirely possible that soft words, soft songs, soft rain pricked her skin with a sweet and salty pain like the tiniest of thorns wedged deep in the ball of your foot. Possible, but apparently bearable, for marry she did.

My mother looked for her slippers. I pushed them closer to her with my feet. She took a short trip to the kitchen for the mandatory sniffing and stirring and boiling water for tea while she was at it. She was a sorceress in the kitchen, and I seldom followed her to that magical kingdom, letting her whip up her concoctions in peace. I was utterly content with the wonderful aromas wafting through the walls. After she returned with a tray stacked with tea, and home-baked beans on toast, she continued:

> On the day of the wedding, Grandmother, in a rare moment of sentiment, asked Sheila if there was anything else she desired to make her wedding day perfect. Sheila requested that instead of instrumental music in the background, she would like to liven the banquet scene with modern Bollywood songs. I don't believe she got that wish. Your grandfather thought classical music was more in keeping with tradition and the solemnity of the occasion.

> Ravi was a stocky looking man with a bulbous nose and a condescending air, eyes hidden behind thick glasses. Average looking you might say. As to how he rated compared to Rohan, you be the judge. Rohan was soft, effeminate with his milky skin and girlish hands. Like men who played the role of women back in Shakespearean days, Rohan's body type

readily lent itself to both male and female parts. That is not to say his sentiments were not manly.

She frowned and searched for the *mot juste* as I smiled inwardly thinking of the transvestites on Venice beach.

Rohan was a sort of insubstantial creature with an idealistic mind who felt deeply and everything he felt was pooled in his eyes. His intelligence translated into thoughtful, compassionate acts, whereas Ravi kept his thoughts selfishly to himself, and as for emotion, he did not inherit any. You might say Ravi's brilliance allowed him to disassociate himself from us mere mortals.

I wish I could say they were happy at first. Their son was a result of their union but conjugation has more to do with sparks of desire than contentment's warm hearth, does it not? I remember asking her once, in a general sort of way, how she was, and she, I must confess, answered with more detail than I was comfortable with, "Rohan treasured me as a thing of beauty and fulfilled my needs even before I knew I had any."

"And Ravi?" I asked, since the subject had now been broached.

All she said was, "I just want some peace."

What kind of an answer is that, Saya, for a twenty-something girl? Already, looking at her face was like looking at a road map thrice folded, frayed from travel, speckled with coffee stains. I went home that day and wept for the Sheila who once could with a mere flick of her inky tresses captivate and change the course of another man's life. Where did she disappear?

Soon after that, they moved to Germany, and we thought, surely a change of scenery would do her good. Europe, I hear, with its crisp air and shimmering lights, chic women, and casually well-dressed men walking with easy strides, murmuring languages elegant and fluid as the Seine can shock you out of your one-dimensional thinking. We were wrong. Sheila became more miserable with each passing month.

I do not know all the details of her life. I am sure she cooked and laundered, dusted and shopped, and did all those busy things one does to beat time at its own game. Perhaps her little boy gave her some joy. But her husband, like the continent of Europe, was a foreign landscape, cold and unremitting, with rigid rules and unknown destinations. It is said he maintained two residences. One, which he shared with her, and one nearer to his place of work, for the sake of convenience. No, he was not an adulterous man, as one might be inclined to think, quite the opposite in fact. I do believe he enjoyed his time away from her, his special hermitage where he could listen to Bach, play solitaire, and drink an occasional gin. And Sheila, she simply sat by the window, like an ignorant girl from a village, with her eyes peeled on the parking lot waiting for signs of life or maybe for someone else to come to her rescue.

I think, at some level Sheila believed she would be rescued, especially as years went by and Rohan still maintained his bachelor's quarters, and no girl ever forgot her scarf in his Spartan rooms. But time moved at the pace of a lizard, and Sheila was going mad with loneliness. There was nothing anyone could do; Ravi was not abusive, just unlovable. Not enough grounds for divorce, although that word was not yet in her vocabulary. She was not motivated to read a book, learn a language, or put on her coat and discover a new country with its imposing architecture, exquisite art, and delectable food and at least meet some interesting people. Lethargically, she stirred her *dal* (lentil soup), cooked packaged macaroni, turned to the mind's gallery, and with the felt tip of her imagination stroked detail upon detail on the artwork of her yellowing pre-marital romance.

Then it was time for her annual visit home, and I believe, Saya, she did visit Rohan unbeknownst to our parents.

"Oh my God! What happened?" I coughed out after I'd finished choking over a piece of toast.

I believe the lovers spent the day crying and celebrating their reunion, but according to what Sheila shared with Harini, (her favorite sister), Rohan would not step outside the bounds of propriety now that she was a married woman. Sheila, at one point, called him a mouse, a loser, and other harsh things, and I imagine the tip of his nose and his ears turned red when he responded, "What purpose will it serve now but to make our parting even more torturous?"

Sheila, throwing caution to the winds asked, "Why do we have to part? Why can't we simply run away, just the two of us?"

He took her head in her hands and shook it like a child's. "Can you live out the rest of your life in this little room? Because outside these walls what you will see is your little boy clamoring for his mother, your own mother hiding her shame behind a permanent white veil, your father with his head not proud or upright but bent with grief, and your sisters turned away from you like a bad smell. Can you survive that? We have to live with the script we are handed, Sheila."

She cooled down then and left but not before extracting a promise he would not refuse to see her on her visits home.

"He was a very practical man despite his poet's heart. He never did marry, Saya. Just languished in his room year after year, making penciled notes in the margins of thick books. That takes some courage too, don't you think?"

Meanwhile luckily or unluckily, it depends on one's perspective, Ravi lost his job and had to return to India where he took a position in a small firm in Delhi.

Sheila was ecstatic. From being a wilted, dried up stick of ginger, she blossomed overnight to her full potential. Her hair thickened and undulated in the wind, her almond eyes shone with excitement, dazzled with powdered magic, her slim waist looked slimmer, her child bearing hips more seductive, her breasts perked up. She looked like one of those tantalizing courtesans invited to entertain in palaces. Her days were spent not cooking or cleaning, for that she had maids, but with building a square mile network of girlfriends in her new neighborhood to gossip, organize teas, and exchange fashion tips. It was as if she had escaped from a desert, and like a camel, she hoarded conversations afraid she might be shipped back.

Mum was getting restless with the tea things still on the bed. Empty cups and saucers belonged in the kitchen sink. Half eaten toast belonged in the garbage. Order gave her life meaning. So of course, the tray had to be cleared post haste before she could resume her story:

> Sheila blossomed, while inversely, her husband became more morose and aloof to the point that one got accustomed to seeing her enter alone behind the two by twos of family gatherings, prayer meetings, or even funerals. When he lost his next job, and the next one, the family elders finally conceded, although privately, that perhaps the Sheila-Ravi match had misfired.
>
> Meanwhile, it was an exciting time for India. Women were no longer left in the sidelines or merely tolerated as teachers, nurses, and social workers. They were entering the workforce, in advertising, pharmaceuticals, hotels, and other industries and doing a good job of it. Bored housewives began experimenting with fashion design, cooking demonstrations, and jewelry trading to supplement their incomes. Inconspicuous little billboards advertising eyebrow threading, waxing, and so on,

appeared almost overnight in practically every apartment building. Businesses made the leap from press to television advertising, and soon electronics, jeans, and make-up became mandatory haves for the have-nots, modeled I may add, by beautiful young women. This subtle unveiling of the traditional woman was viewed first as disturbing, then acceptable, and at last entrepreneurial, even by those as conservative as your grandmother!

Sheila too established her own one-room beauty salon and made a little nest egg that knocked the condescension right off her husband's stuck up nose. Depressed at her success, he comforted himself with overeating, and then, alarmed at his bulging waistline, the vain man began walking miles on end, obsessively. As such, he was either too full or too tired even to attend to the son, who once interested him because he looked and sounded so much like him. And so they lived as a family under the same roof, uncommunicative, indifferent, and disillusioned.

Mum heaved a sigh, and I could tell by her expression

that her attention had drifted to something else, and she shifted gears. "The day my father passed away was the darkest day of my life, Saya. He was my lighthouse, my reason to hope, keeping the harsh glare of penury out of my eyes, long after I was given away in marriage," she admitted and then forced her mind back to the unfolding saga of Sheila:

> For Sheila though, the news was not all bad. A germ of an idea grew in her mind, as if the demise of the ferocious old man made the challenges ahead seem easier to surmount. Her son was about to graduate from high school, old enough, in her mind, to handle the sober realities of life.
>
> "I will leave Ravi," she confessed to Harini.
>
> "I will marry Rohan and move in with him."
>
> Whereas once, the very idea would not have made it past Sheila's lips, Harini merely nodded sorrowfully.
>
> "Yes," she agreed. "Life is short. You deserve some happiness."
>
> On the eve of the son's graduation, Sheila was nervous as a cat about to birth kittens. Her son,

she knew, planned to celebrate into the morning with friends. She'd decided she would confront her husband the same evening when he was likely to be comatose from all the celebratory snack foods after the graduation and would not venture out of the house, giving her ample time to discuss her decision. She felt assured things would eventually work out fine for all concerned, except for one niggling worry – she hadn't broached the idea with Rohan yet. Surely, she could convince him now, she thought and, wiping her palms on her *kurta*, focused on the speeches droning on, occasionally craning her neck this way and that to see if her husband had made it to the ceremony after all. Of course, he hadn't. *The no good, selfish creep,* she thought with righteous indignation, *I am right to be rid of him.*

The three floors to her apartment seemed three miles long that day. For some reason, her left leg felt twitchy and her lower back was giving her trouble. She made it upstairs at last and even before she took the keys out to open the door, a sickening feeling of loss made the whites of her eyes whiter.

Ravi was home. "What's the matter?" she asked, seeing the look on his face.

"Your cousin, Rohan," he said and she thudded to the floor.

Rohan had contracted a fairly common form of meningitis and had complained of a severe headache to a colleague, and then he was just gone. He had some cash and bonds he left for his unmarried sisters. For Sheila as well, he left a fair amount of money tucked inside a note written on onionskin paper in beautiful, practiced calligraphy.

Mother was quiet so long I thought she was done with the story. Then she murmured: "Rohan told me once he might die without Sheila. It seems he spent the better part of his life preparing for that day." ♦

The Thief of St. Mary's

Beautiful angel, my guardian so mild, tenderly guide me, for I am thy child.
- ***The Sunday School Hymn Book***
("Sisters of the Notre Dame," 1907)

Feeling a little bit like Red Riding Hood, I trudged off to Grandma's house to visit with various aunts, uncles, and cousins. Grandma herself, scarcely 4' 4" in height, her pendulous south facing breasts skimming her belly, an odd figure unrelieved by humor or wit, had passed away a few years before, stubbornly outliving her husband, a son-in law, and two stepchildren.

Poor Aunt Sheila. Poor Rohan. If only my grandparents had let them marry. I am a deep believer in the power of positive thinking and am quite convinced love can fix anything, even meningitis. Anyway, it was those two I was thinking about when on the way over, I bumped, quite ungracefully, into a woman carrying a tote full of fruit and smelling a little like mothballs.

"Sorry!" I grunted.

"It's okay," she muttered and bent down to retrieve a banana. I bent down too and this time we bumped noses rather hard, making her yell, "Ouch," and jump back.

"Sorry again …I was just trying to help."

She sighed a martyred sigh, and it was as she moved her hand away from her aching nose that I recognized the girl I knew from my school days.

"Mona! Is that you?"

"Yes. Hi," she said, not quite as excited.

"What are you doing in these parts?"

"I live here, remember," she gestured in the direction of a row of buildings smeared with the oily composition of dust, fumes, salt, and other unknown deposits blowing in from the ocean on the west and the suburbs along the east.

"Did you not move when you married?"

I'd forgotten her husband's name and let him hang in the air like an ellipsis. She sighed again, and I held back another apology, not wanting to sound like a broken record.

"Saya," she said, "let's go sit on that bench if you have time. We can catch up." Without waiting for my reply she angled herself toward it.

Mona cleared the chalky stuff filmed over the bench with her hand and sat down, pulling her *kurta* under her seat purposefully. She seemed to be collecting her thoughts. As she organized her fruit about her, her lashes fluttered and branched, her lips curled to a soft smile, and a glimpse of the talcum fresh loveliness that once captivated an entire school finally peered from under the puffiness of her eyes and the folds of her neck. Time does not efface; it simply recomposes, I thought.

Perhaps she sensed that I was staring, for Mona continued to smile her mischievous smile for a moment or two before she asked, "Saya, this takes me back to another moment in time when we sat together on a bench. Do you remember?"

I was confused. We were in school together through tenth grade. Surely we must have sat down together plenty of times. "In class, do you mean?"

"No," she shook her head. "On a bench, during recess the day the entire school snubbed me, and I sat outside with my solitary lunch box staring at my watch, literally counting the minutes before I could get back to class and bury my face in a history lesson. I don't think I breathed the entire time."

I felt my face burn. Why would Mona bring this incident up now after all these years?

"It was a long time ago," I finally ventured. "We were just kids."

"I wasn't. A kid I mean. I was quite mature as I recall being told over and over by a number of people."

"We are the same age, Mona," I said, a little irritated. I looked at my watch.

"I remember when the nun finally discovered it was me," Mona muttered, almost to herself, moving into a quiet reminiscing tone:

> Sister Antoinette wanted to see a final rehearsal

before you all went out to perform *A Comedy of Errors* in the inter-school competition. Someone, I think it was the science teacher, suggested it would be a good idea to perform before an audience - "It would make all of you more comfortable for the final show."

So the whole school squeezed together in the auditorium. When everyone was seated, it occurred to me there was no one in the classrooms. I sneaked out, holding my stomach as if I was in pain. Instead of going to the bathroom, I sneaked into the nearest classroom. There were several raincoats hanging in the back of the room. I put my hands into the pocket of one. Nothing. In another, I found some gum. I tossed it into the bin and stuck my hand in another coat. I found cash in one pocket. In the other pocket, I found a copper bracelet. I took them both. Hastily, I thrust the stuff into my pocket, turned around, and nearly fainted in fright. Inches away from my face stood Sister Rose in her black habit, the whites of her eyes gleaming, her cane thrust in the air like a curse.

"So, it's you. The thief of St Mary's," she hissed.

Then she put out her hand. Still in shock, I wasn't sure what that meant. Viciously she tugged at my dress and dug her fingers in my pockets. They felt like claws, trying to get at my skin.

She retrieved my loot and said, "Come with me."

Of course, I followed. There was such a gleam in her eyes. So triumphant, as if she had singlehandedly nabbed the chainsaw murderer. I was taken to the principal's office and made to confess everything. She wrote a note for my parents. I had to bring back all the stolen stuff. Bangles and watches, rings, and cash stolen over the past few weeks. Probably not worth much, we were kids after all, but it seemed like a lot at the time.

"You are probably wondering why I did it."

The principal asked me that very question. She said I was the last girl in the school she'd expect to find stealing. It was a filthy, odious thing to do, and she didn't understand my behavior.

I told her that was why I did it, "Because nobody would suspect. Thieves are either poor, or ugly and unpopular. I am not poor, I am beautiful and the darling of the school. Everyone wants to be my friend."

I have to say she was quite shocked. She told me stealing was not my worst crime. Pride was. She would teach me a lesson. The next day every single student from kindergarten upwards knew of my sin, and I was summarily ostracized. I may as well have been publicly lynched. Being shunned felt so harsh.

It went on like that for a few days. During class it was okay. It was at recess that I felt like a ghost at a Christmas party. Then one day, *you* came, Saya, and sat down next to me. Just like that. We didn't talk much, but we exchanged sandwiches. I had cheese. You had tomato. I remember licking my fingers, your sandwich tasted so good! Or perhaps I felt hungry again after a very long time. I wanted to tell you, I've never forgotten your sensitivity, your kindness. Your mother raised you well.

I shrugged uncomfortably, hoping that might be the

end of Mona's sad story, but she went on, almost as if I was not even there:

> A week later, the principal called me to her office again. She asked me if I had learned my lesson. What was I going to say ... no? I said, "Yes, indeed."
>
> Then she said, "Now, I want to know the *real* reason why you would resort to stealing when all you had to do was ask your parents for the things you desire. Do they not give you treats from time to time?"
>
> She wouldn't let me go until she got to the truth. She had those piercing blue eyes like the nurse in *One flew over the Cuckoo's Nest*. So, finally I told her. I said, "I'm a bad person anyway, so doing one more bad thing didn't seem to matter."
>
> She asked me why I thought I was a bad person. That's when I told her about Mr. Mathis.

"The algebra teacher?" I asked. "What did he have to do with anything?"

Mona looked at me, her eyes hooded. Oh bloody hell,

I thought. This was turning out to be quite the after school special. Literally. She continued her story:

> Mr. Mathis held an extra class twice a week after school hours for those of us who had trouble with algebra and geometry. One evening, he cornered me at the bus stop and said he didn't think I was making fast enough progress. He said he would take time off his busy schedule to tutor me separately if I was serious. He implied I might fail the exam if I didn't work harder. What was I going to say? Of course, I agreed to see him.
>
> Things went well at first. Then he got increasingly moody and ill tempered. When I couldn't solve a math problem, he made a paper jet of my sheet and flung it into the bin. I was quite upset. When he saw I was afraid, he apologized. He said he was having marriage troubles and felt he could confide in me because I was mature for my age. I was flattered and tried to look as understanding as I could, even though I was dying to go home. My mother was baking a cake that night, and I was afraid there'd be none left for me if I

lingered too long.

He began crying! Great big tear drops rained down his cheeks and onto my shirtfront. Yes, he held me close and cried on my shoulder. I was petrified. I remember patting him tentatively on his head like a puppy. His hair was greasy and made my fingers smell of coconut oil.

Mathis seduced me. And I let him. How strange it seems in retrospect, Saya. A man of no fame, neither handsome nor rich. He took everything from me yet implied I owed him. He gave me nothing yet suggested I was getting more than my share. Confused with his logic, fearful of being found out, my body grew slack, unresisting, and finally quite malleable. An occasional word of praise from him at just the right moment, and it no longer felt like abuse. It felt almost ... reassuring.

Meanwhile I was not doing much better at math. My mother mistook the sexually sedated look in my eyes for laziness and decided I did not need to be tutored any longer. She said, "Either one applies oneself, or one does not.

Clearly you have no intention to, so I'd rather use your tuition money on your sister's cooking lessons." I had to agree.

Besides there was a boy in my neighborhood who I found infinitely more attractive than old Mr. Mathis, who never took me anywhere where the lighting was not dim. All we ever had was fresh lime soda. He would laugh and say, "Princesses don't eat," and I would grin weakly, my stomach rumbling. But Mathis was furious when I told him I had to quit class. He accosted me in the library, the church, once even in the ladies room and threatened me at every turn. He said he'd tell the principal I was a bad girl who made him cheat on his wife, that I used my wiles to seduce older men. And so on and on until I was as thoroughly disgusted with myself as he apparently was with me. That's when I began stealing.

I shared all this with Principal Augusta. She was very quiet for a while. Then she thanked me for being frank. She said I was not a bad girl, although it wouldn't hurt to pull down my hemline. She said Mr. Mathis was the one who was bad; it was he who had wronged me and that he would be punished. She spoke to me a little about predators. She also said any relationship that is not out in the open is base at the core. She told me not to be so quick to override my own instincts. She said some of the usual nun-like things too about chastity and penance and all that, but that was the gist of it.

Anyway, that was the year Mathis got axed. I'm willing to bet he's back on his feet and continues to exploit other children. Evil hovers over such men like stench over a gutter. I learned a lot from Principal Augusta, but I also learned something *about* Principal Augusta that day: she might be a nun, but she certainly knew a lot about the outside world. Also, she was willing to give credence to the words of a child. When I got up to leave, she actually thanked me. I've always wondered why.

"Mona, I'm pretty sure she learned a lot from you too that day. But tell me, why did you not confide in any of us?"

"Confide what? That Mathis was following me around like a bloodhound rubbing his nose and sticking his tongue in places I washed in the lavatory? Who would believe me?

I was doomed to secrecy. Anyway, in the final year of school, he was gone, and my stealing or kleptomania or whatever it was stopped of its own accord. I mean I did not just stop for fear of the principal's wrath. And thanks to you, other girls began drifting to my bench at lunchtime, and pretty soon Mona the Thief was replaced once more by Mona of the Milky Skin and Melon-fresh Mona and Peaches-n-cream Mona and…"

"I got it. You are beginning to sound like a smoothie!" I was suddenly overcome with hilarity and burst out laughing. Mona laughed as well, and soon I no longer had to look past the watermarks of time to see the old Mona. She sat before me pink with pleasure, aglow with the happiness that bubbles like a hot spring warming the very air within the perimeter of two friends exchanging confidences.

After we had both quieted down a little, she said, "You wondered what I was doing back here. I am divorced, Saya. My marriage did not work out."

I rearranged my features and nodded soberly.

> Soon after high school, where I will have you know, I did passably well in all subjects including algebra, -- I met Manish, my ex-husband. It was on a very hot day at the World

Trade Fair. I was holding up one of those gorgeous tribal skirts to my waist and admiring myself in the full-length mirror behind the overly talkative salesman. Manish came up behind me and simply stood there staring at my reflection. I remember thinking, what an ugly looking man when I saw the bracelet on his hairy wrist. It was made of solid gold and quite mesmerizing.

Within the week, he came knocking at our door. He proposed marriage and to my parents' surprise - they were willing to wait a few years, since I was so young - I agreed.

Years later, he accused me of marrying him for his money. "So what?" I retorted. "Did you not marry me for my body? Surely it was not my numinous spirit that made your upper lip bead that day at the Trade Fair?"

"Show me a human being, Saya, and I will show you the craving that upsets his digestion, be it wealth or youth or power or artistic legacy. It is my firm belief we are covetous by nature," she said before continuing her story:

In any event, in the first few years of our marriage, we were really quite happy. He thought I was extraordinarily beautiful, and I enjoyed his attentions. To my credit, I never made him *feel* ugly. I simply focused on the gold bracelet on his wrist, his starched collars, his expensive aftershave, and the smart way he was saluted every time we entered or exited a 5-star hotel. Every once in a while at a party or some corporate event, I would hear a suppressed catcall, an occasional snigger, a cruel remark behind our backs, such as "Beauty and the Beast" or "Wow, look at what money can buy," but I paid them no heed. He did not ever appear to notice and I, well I didn't really care as long as I was cast as Beauty. Then one day, quite by accident, I discovered he was having an affair.

I tried to cover my startled expression by burrowing into my bag for a piece of caramel candy. I found two and offered Mona one. She sucked on it ruminatively for a few moments and then carried on, seemingly transported to a new place:

You know the shooting game Bullseye in which players shoot handguns at a paper target at fixed distances? Seven hundred students and faculty used my heart for target practice over a decade ago. Of course, they did not use handguns. Only their taunting eyes and cold shoulders. When Manish cheated on me, it dawned on me, at last, that there are no coincidences in life. The stealing and the subsequent humiliations were the prelims. This was life's final exam prepared especially for me. Would I keel over or would I survive?

For a few months, I teetered on the edge. I was in turn mute, depressed, cowering in dark corners, contemplating self-injury, not to mention death by sleeping pills or drowning. Then one day my mood changed, my very complexion turned black so that, like the goddess Kali, I wanted to annihilate everyone in sight, especially Manish and the other woman.

It was in the latter frame of mind that I went to see her. Don't ask me how I found out who she was and where she lived. Suffice it to say that I did find her. I rang the doorbell, and she let me in. I thought she was the maid. I remember asking, "Is madam in?"

"Come in, Mona. I'm Rasna," she said, sweet as pie. I did not apologize for mistaking her for a servant. That would have changed the whole tone of the meeting, wouldn't it? Besides, you know what they say, if you look like a duck and walk like a duck … If I had not been so full of rage, Saya, I might actually have found the situation funny. They looked so much alike! Like Cinderella's ugly sisters or, in this case, like an ugly brother and sister. She was dark like him, her teeth stuck out like his, as if ready to chomp on a bone, her hair hung down to her hips, long but also rough and stringy. And if one were willing to get closer to her face, you'd see she even sported a hint of a moustache, just like Manish!

"What does he see in you?" I found myself wondering aloud. Again, I did not apologize for my rudeness.

She did not answer immediately but handed me a glass of tepid water from the sink. "I wondered that myself when he first asked me out," she said finally when we were seated across from each other in her tacky little living room. I could see from the pillow tucked hastily away, she used the divan as a bed at night.

"Manish and I talk as equals. And we talk a lot, sometimes through the night. He shares everything with me. His life, his hopes, his dreams."

Pain shot through me like a dagger. She saw that and continued unfazed, "Do you have anything you talk about other than your kitty parties?"

"No," I said venomously. "We don't talk. We make love at night. Sometimes three times a night."

I thought that would hush her up, but she merely flared her nostrils and stated, "I know he uses protection. Would you like to know why?"

I was so incensed I could barely sit still. I stood up and paced about. How did she know about the protection? Why would he mention it?

Then she changed the subject and started shooting questions at me like a bloody cowboy with a pistol at her hip.

"Did you know that Manish was an adopted child? From the look on your face, I gather that you did not.

"Did you know that he seeks out impoverished families and donates dowry money to eligible women every year? No, you did not.

"You see you are a self-absorbed, vain creature who does little more than lend a dab of *attar* to his already beautiful personality."

Then just as I thought I could not feel more humiliated, she said, "He's been waiting for you to mature as a human being before he can impregnate you. He wants a *real* mother for his child, not one you admire in the centerfold of a magazine then stick it in the wicker basket by the toilet."

That was the last straw, Saya. I lunged forward and hissed and spit on her like a cat. She didn't move, letting the glob of spittle sit on her chin and thread down her neck. But by the time I reached home, it was I who felt like scum. Then I thought, wait a minute, I am the wronged party here, not Manish and certainly not Rasna! You do not close a rift in your marriage by forging a covert path to another's bed. Sister Augusta had taught me well. The next day I asked him for a divorce. The relief was quite mutual.

Mona stretched out her hand. It took me a second to realize she was asking for another candy. I gave her one and stood up slowly. "I'm invited to lunch," I pointed at my grandmother's building with my thumb, "but now that I know you are here to stay, we will meet again."

Mona smiled. "Not for long Saya. I'm getting remarried."

I sat down again.

"I've met a good man. Not too rich, not too plain," she smiled at my expression, "but the best part is, he wants children, at once!"

The puffiness under her eyes subsided as if by magic, and in place of fine lines hope lit up her eyes like the night-blooming Cereus, leaving me breathless. Her cheeks too took on a warm hue, and her whole being seemed suffused with a sort of maternal glow. My eyes went to her thighs spread slightly apart so that her knees jutted out at an angle and her feet formed a V. Her *kurta* billowed a little below her suspiciously full breasts. Was that a bump? Or was it the way the wind filled the *kurta* just then?

I averted my face, not willing to follow that thought and asked instead, rising determinedly this time, "By the way, do you remember Ami? I'd like to visit her."

Mona's face fell, "Yes, as a matter of fact, I have her number. Do get in touch with her, Saya. You know, she was in an accident."

She scribbled on the back of a receipt and rushed off before I could mouth a question. ♦

The Homemaker

Time may wash away your dreams, but not your ability to stay afloat.

- Jaya

All my obligatory visits were over, and I looked forward to spending the rest of my time with Mum and a few special friends. The next day, however, we received some sad news. My Aunt Mohini from my father's side of the family had passed away. Mother absorbed the news with little more than a widening of the eyes and a serious air. Out of respect, we did not put the TV on or plan a dinner that may be construed as overly festive or one that included dessert or a non-vegetarian meal. She did not deem it appropriate to wear make-up or go shopping for a few days either. It was the height of summer, and as the days stretched interminably, I was beginning to get restless.

A little impatiently, I suggested we go down and sit on the park benches. I needed some air and a change of scenery; I was going cuckoo in the cage-like apartment. Mum nodded understandingly and went in to find her slippers. She was extremely tolerant, even amused, of the airs she assumed I'd acquired in America.

The park, although no bigger than my backyard back in New Jersey, still conveyed an impression of expanse. Kids flitted about like summer blooms supervised by moms ensconced on benches set little more than a foot apart so that several conversations surged and ebbed obtrusively over our heads.

Slowly, my mother peeled an orange and offered me a segment. We sat in companionable silence for a bit until she sighed and wiped her mouth, giving me the rest of the orange as if she'd suddenly lost her appetite. "How time flies," she said, shaking her head from side to side as if disagreeing with herself.

"Are you thinking about Mohini Auntie?"

She frowned and admitted, "Not really. I was thinking about my life. So much has happened that is inexplicable. I'm glad it all came about when I was young. Surely I could not have survived such struggle in later years."

I did not answer. I knew what she was thinking of, knew it well by now, but if it helped her to repeat herself, who was I to interrupt? She began:

> I remember stepping into my husband's house after our marriage ceremony. It was little more than a garret you know, Saya. There was no electricity, no running water, and no wall separating the living area from the sleeping or dining, so that the entire family lay on mats at night, in various corners of the one room, covering our modesty with bed sheets.
>
> The henna had not yet dried on my hands, but I was expected to take on the chores, cooking, washing, sweeping the floors, caring for the little ones – his one brother and two sisters. I did not have a mother in-law; apparently she died during childbirth, though I'm convinced

she willed herself to die, if such a thing is possible.

You know how resilient I am, how active. I was not afraid of hard work, thanks to my stepmother. But what made my heart stop in the middle of flipping bread on a coal fire - If you ever wonder what hell is like, Saya, try sitting by an open flame at the height of a Delhi summer - was the fear that my father might forget about me. Partition was upon us. How easy it would be for him to lose himself in reestablishing his many businesses amidst a newly formed government and managing the complaints of his contumacious wife and the marriages of my younger sisters. After all, there was no one he knew in this Independent India. A lifetime of connections were cast into the incinerator and reduced to ashes as time marched inexorably on. Now, it was up to him to recreate a semblance of order, balance, and optimism in the future. How alone he must have felt and yet how bravely he handled himself.

My fears were compounded as I did not get the

customary invitation to visit my parents within a month of being married. Perhaps stepmother did not think it necessary.

"Too much was going on," she later justified her negligence. "It was partition time, after all."

I wanted to know more about her new living arrangements. "What was your father-in-law like?" I asked.

Mum shuddered. "Like no man I'd ever come across," she answered, and told me more:

> As you know, my father's home was open to the entire clan, and I was entrusted with the responsibility of making guests comfortable. Hence, I was used to the company of adults and could tell almost at hello, the personality of the guest: this one will be a glutton, this one a snorer or a bore or a talker. And I was always right. Your Aunt Dina would swear by my instincts, but *this* man, I honestly could not fathom.
>
> My father-in-law could sweep you off your feet with the breadth of his knowledge, mesmerize you with his singing, and fill you with awe when he came out of the bath resplendent in

white and gold.

But there was something foul about him. Imagine for a moment, Saya, if our beautiful ancient scriptures were desecrated, or our serving bowls used as spittoons, how would that make you feel?

That was my father-in-law. A disgusting man who fell on his food like a hyena on a carcass, who charmed women with his Aryan looks and repelled them with profanities, who was polite to you in private and then humiliated you in public, who resisted the temptation to make money but had no problem ridding you of yours.

I remember when I was at last granted a visit home. My father gave me presents – cash, jewelry, and clothes. When I returned after a three-week visit, I was asked to unpack in the center of the room in front of an audience. My bags, with my underthings and all, were emptied and turned over like a sack of potato chips, every crumb extracted! I never saw those presents again. Still, it was my duty to serve my father-in-law, and I did so, but with a wall around my heart as thick and constant as a pillar.

The worst of it was that your father grew up wanting to be just like him.

Uncomfortable, I averted my face. My father was long gone, and I did not want to resurrect him. "Was he never nice to you then, considering all you did, raising his other children and giving *him* grandchildren?"

Mother considered. He enjoyed my cooking, I suppose. He died of tuberculosis, you know, and I nursed him night and day, burning every rag he touched, washing his garments separately, and feeding him with my own hands.

On his deathbed, he called me aside and said, "At least I know my children will be looked after."

That was the first and last time he came close to paying me a compliment, yet it made me so immeasurably happy. Because of this one miserable, miserly acknowledgement, I wept though the night, vowing to remember only his eloquence, his love for poetry, and the pleasure he took in classical music. I also vowed that night I would take better care of his children than my own. I like to think that I have.

"You *did* take care of them," I said.

And again my mother smiled her enigmatic smile.

"Tell me about Dad's youngest sister, Rani. I know she has a special place in your heart. What was she like as a child?" I asked, hoping to divert the conversation to a more cheerful path.

Mum relaxed. "Rani?" Her face lit up like a candle sparking laugh lines from the corners of her eyes, and she relaxed into the story:

> Such a pretty girl. Such a loving girl, always rubbing against me like a kitten, wanting to be picked up and held and fed with my fingers. I had very little time for leisure, but all she had to do was hold out her arms, and I would gather her up, whether I was dusty from flour, covered in soap suds, or slick with vegetable oil. It all started when I saw her one evening facing the wall, surreptitiously drawing little star shapes with a piece of charcoal. "Why aren't you downstairs playing with your little

friends?" I asked.

She burst into tears. "I don't want to. They tease me and scare me."

I picked her up and held her in my lap. "What do they say to you?"

"They say that now that my brother is married, you are our mother. But since you are not my *real* mother, you will be cruel, like a wicked witch, and hurt me with a poker when I'm asleep."

I comforted her then. I told her I didn't own a poker, and if I ever so much as raised my voice to her, all she had to do was say the name of God thrice and reduce me to ashes. She believed me, of course; she was barely three at the time, and I admit she has been my favorite since then. She has lovely green eyes with flecks of gold, and when she gets emotional, you can see all the colors of the rainbow reflected in them.

I watched Rani's development like a hawk, not letting the neighborhood kids or your father's family influence her too strongly. Her father would send her to the kitchen to help me with my chores, as with all men in those days, he wanted to turn his daughters into docile little housewives by the age of fourteen. Instead I would give her a used copy of *Grimm's Fairytales* I found in the bazaar and ask her to read them aloud to me. When she was done reading, I would treat her to a slice of pound cake, which I baked using a tin can for a tandoor, Saya, and milk flavored with almonds. There, sitting on a high stool in that windowless oil and grime encrusted kitchen, I somehow managed to fill her head with snow covered peaks, green valleys, red apples as large as melons, princes in top hats, and princesses in flowing chiffons. *That* was reality, I told her without so many words. The flytrap that we lived in was but a dream. Some day she would wake up and live her true life.

When she turned thirteen, I showed her some grooming tricks. I taught her how to wear her hair so that it did not look flat and dull. I stole food money and bought her some deodorant, a razor, some cold cream, and other feminine accouterments, carefully hidden from the eagle eyes of her father who disapproved of pretty much everything but often used cologne and had a weakness for silk scarves himself. Being a good girl, she still wanted to help out, so I taught her to cook, which she now does magnificently, but would not let her near any of the non-creative, menial tasks like sweeping and scouring.

"You will have servants when you grow up," I said. "For now, focus on your music lessons (she had a beautiful voice), do some accounting, and cook us something special now and then."

I wanted her to think, act, and live her life like a mistress, not get brainwashed by the narrow minded, self-righteous creatures dwelling in shanties, rubbing their overfed bellies, expounding about modesty, self-sacrifice, a woman's role, and other rubbish.

Rani was deathly afraid of marrying the man we chose for her. He was handsome, wealthy, and quite the man about town. She was artless, unaccustomed to the society of men outside her immediate family, and did not know that whole evenings could be spent making small talk and eating bite-sized meals, but I told her she would be all right. She was beautiful and wore her beauty like a flower, not the cold glint of a jewel. Her ways were gentle, and her mind was quick. It is a rare man who can resist the combination. She agreed to the marriage at last and today, as you know, has three sons of her own.

It may have been tough at first. She did hint that her life was a series of parties where very little was said and much was implied, and where she stood out like a weed in a field of lilies. By then I had so many problems of my own and could not be terribly supportive. I told her to give him time, he would learn to appreciate her soon enough. Superficiality can interest a man for only so long, but if she felt herself lacking in some way, she ought to do something about it! As always, she took my words to heart, went back to school, and got a master's degree in languages. Her self-confidence restored at last, she took to helping him with their many businesses and enjoys an enviable position in the community today.

> I am so pleased that she has everything I dreamed of for her. A beautiful home in the verdant valley of Shimla where the flow of ideas between both sexes is encouraged, and where, surrounded by friends, business associates, and all the silks in the world at her disposal, she still maintains her unaffected manner and proudly demonstrates her respect for this "not real mother" in her faded cotton saris and her kitchen-reddened hands.

"She'd better show you respect," I said, "or else, I'll go after her with a poker myself." We both laughed at the reference.

"You remind me of her sometimes, Saya, except you have darker skin and are not so sweet-tempered."

"Gee! Thanks!" I said, but did not take any offence. It was just my mother's way.

"Tell me about dad's brother, Aunt Mohini's husband. What was he like?"

Mum conveyed her impatience with a flick of her fingers, but launched into a new story, spurred by my interest:

> He was tiresome, overly talkative, and quite

naïve when he was young. I'm not sure what gives one the idea that the world owes you a living just because you are good looking. Beauty is a gift, Saya, not of your own making. It says nothing about you except there is a very good chance you might turn out vain, arrogant, and a glutton for flattery.

Your uncle was slight, with a head of golden curls and beautiful, expressive eyes. He played the flute every time he fell in love, and he fell in love often. A ribbon swinging on a braid, a *kurta* rustling in the breeze, a dimple surfacing on a cheek, all the stuff of black and white cinema in fact, shaped his dreams. He lived for these provocations, and it was all I could do to divert his mind to other things, like getting a B.A. degree and making a good living.

When he continued to miss classes and did not seriously look for a job as an alternative, I finally used my half-baked psychology. I handed him his clothes, hand washed and pressed as requested, then took him aside, and said, "Do you know, when I was in college the girls used to say the one quality they most admired in men was the ability to take charge, become good providers, show them who is boss." I think my words did have some effect on him. He did well in his finals and actually got a clerical job in some sort of manufacturing plant.

A couple of years later, we went about the business of finding him a bride. He saw Mohini and immediately fell in love with her dusky looks and open smile. You know, Saya, the elders tell us the first step a bride takes in your home determines the shape of her husband's fortune. That is why we greet her at the door with a prayer and a blessing. Mohini stepped over the threshold but not, unfortunately, with fortune on her side. Your uncle lost his job and was turned down by many other establishments. In those days, there was no one to direct these young men, show them how to behave during a job interview, and how to demonstrate skill, obedience, confidence, and humility all at the same time, in the right proportion. Your uncle would march in with his customary nonchalance, his this-is-who-I-am, take-it-or-leave-it attitude. Obviously, it did not work. He grew alarmingly thin and quite the angry young man.

There was no money coming in. In desperation, I wrote to my brother and he offered your uncle a job in his new factory. He would have to live away from home and come on occasional visits. Mohini would stay back with us. That scenario did not work out too well, at all. She was brash and immature. I realize now she was young, probably missed her husband, and did not know how to behave in this large, unwieldy, unknown family. Also, she was the daughter of a machinist, the labor class, which would not be so bad if she had a generous heart or a thinking mind. Her cooking left much to be desired as well, so she became the butt of jokes at the dinner table. I would glare at the family to leave her alone, but I think she didn't realize I was on her side and soon vented much of her misery and frustration on me. Occasionally, I admonished her; I did not have time for her whining, and she either pouted and sulked, and did not talk for days or flew into a rage, the likes of which I had never in my life seen. I recently read about people who are bipolar, Saya. I did not know about it then, but now I am convinced it was the disease that plagued her mind.

"Because she threw tantrums?" I asked.

"That and for several other reasons," Mum said, sighing. I thought for a moment she would not continue the story, but soon she gathered herself and went on:

> I sent her to visit her husband, thinking it would be good for the two of them and it would be a nice change for us too, not having her hover over the house like a dark cloud, but that plan turned out disastrously.

What is marriage Saya, if not mutual respect, compromise, and the instinctive need to ensure the happiness and enhance the stature of your better half? Neither Mohini nor your uncle had the necessary qualifications for a good marriage. Her mood swings and his arrogance combined for such intense drama in his little apartment that neighbors began complaining. Finally, he sent her back to us, saying she was too much of a distraction.

Mohini returned and seemed a little subdued for a while. She had been trying to have a baby and was finally expecting her first child. Coincidentally, I was pregnant at the same time with my fourth, your baby brother, and for a short time, we actually became friends, laughing over cravings, knitting socks and blankets, and exchanging gossip late in the afternoons when you were all at school and there was relative peace in the house. Then I had my baby, a healthy sweet boy, and Mohini lost hers. All hell broke loose. I don't think she grieved as much for the loss of her infant as the fact that I had mine, alive and well. It was frightening how she raged, Saya, beating her breasts, gnashing her teeth like one possessed and screaming like a banshee, "It's your fault, you child-eater," and other wild imprecations. I was actually scared for my life! We finally sedated her. In time, she grew quiet, and I had her sent off to Rani's, who was pregnant as well. I told Mohini if she lovingly and devotedly cared for Rani during her pregnancy, God would favor her with a child. She listened. In time she had children after all.

Mum grew silent for a bit. Just then, Maina, our upstairs neighbor, stopped by. We made small talk but I was eager to hear more about my aunt and uncle.

"And uncle?" I prompted as soon as Maina left.

Mum nodded and took me back, once again, to a lost time:

> His situation was as bad as ever. At work, he was rude, did not think anything of spontaneously singing or playing the flute and disrupting work, but what was infinitely worse was this compulsion to show his bosses, in this case my dear brother, in a bad light, and soon it became evident that his job was in jeopardy.
>
> My brother called to let me know he was going to fire your uncle. I pleaded with him, I said, "He's young; he will learn." Then he gave me a blow-by-painful-blow of your uncle's shenanigans. Apparently he was turning into quite the rabble-rouser, riling the workers against the dictator class, as he called them. He formed a Labor Union and fraternized with them, even living among the workers in their shanties to demonstrate his loyalty towards them. He began selling tea and bread in a makeshift stall adjacent to the factory to show how poorly the boss treated a member of his

own family, that he had to run a business on the side. It was beyond embarrassing. It was horrific! I was so ashamed I could barely get the words out to apologize to my brother and told him simply to fire him at once.

When your uncle returned home, I told him he had a month to pack his bags and leave town. Find a job, live on the street, do whatever he had to, I was cutting him off. He was shocked, of course, and quite disenchanted. He said I would not treat him thus if he were my real son and that I did not truly love him. I told him it was *exactly* how I would treat *any* son of mine. That someday he would realize the subtle difference between a loving act and a punitive one.

It took twenty years, but he has realized the difference at last.

"How do you know he has?" I asked.

"When your father passed away, your uncle finally showed his face at our door. We did not really speak to each other of the past. Where do you begin after all these years? But it was all written in his eyes, and a few weeks after he left he sent me a present.

"What was it?"

"A washing machine."

I studied my mother silently, nearly throwing my hands in the air with a "pshaw!" A *washer* for all the years she'd spent nurturing him, getting him married, and ensuring he took responsibility for his actions and become a real man! Of course, I'd forgotten how well she could read my face.

"It was a gesture, Saya. He owed me nothing. Love is a voluntary act, a not-for-profit venture. Anything else is just a transaction," she said, using my shoulder to hoist herself.

It was time for her favorite religious program on television. As we headed to the elevator, I gently reminded her that I would be spending most of the next day with friends, for there were only a few days left of my visit. She nodded agreeably. ♦

Oceanfront Property

Whose ocean is it anyway?

- Ami

I found a phone number on the back of a receipt and remembered Mona's words as she scribbled it for me. More out of curiosity than anything else, I called Ami and asked if we could meet. She sounded so glad to hear from me I almost felt guilty I hadn't been in touch before. Anyway, I had a couple of hours, so I asked Mum if I could help out in the kitchen. She gave me a platter of greens. I was to divest them from their stems, wash them thoroughly, and then blend them in the food processor along with wheat flour and water. She'd roll out the resultant dough for flat bread. It was her way of making us eat our veggies. I looked distastefully at the fenugreek leaves stacked higher than a mound of hay and then rubbed one gingerly between thumb and index finger. It felt grainy. I looked at my hands. I could make thumbprints with the dirt marks.

"Yay for organic," I mouthed sarcastically and went to the sink to wash them.

"You don't wash first, you de-stem first," said the Controlling One seconds after I'd begun hosing them down.

"What difference does it make? Stem them first or after?" I asked irritably and went on with it.

Of course, when they were wet and squishy it was difficult to pull the leaves off, but I wasn't about to admit my mistake. Nonchalantly I walked to the open balcony and placed the ragged platter on the floor hoping to dry the greens under a soft pool of light. I came in for a break. Kitchen work was hard. Then I heard her apocalyptic shriek.

"Oh my God, what now?" I cried.

"You kept the greens out there! Look what you've done!"

The platter was overturned. Not such a catastrophe in itself until you saw the crow droppings liberally dotting each stem.

"Ugh!" I pulled on a scarf and left the apartment before I was subjected to any more histrionics.

"Going to Ami's," I shouted, shutting the door behind me.

I walked along the beach, keeping my neck craned toward the water to get the full effect of the cool mist rising heavenward. My lips felt salty, my hair attached itself to the back of my neck, and my blouse filled up with air so that I looked like a balloon on legs.

How lucky to still own oceanfront property, I thought as the calm rhythmic beating of the water against rocks, the delicious 80-degree warmth, the droning of boats in the distance, all nature in fact, conspired to rock me into a state of infant-like stupor until I looked at my watch and the fizz went out of me. Time for my meeting.

Ami lived on the first floor of an obscenely tall apartment building that was once an odd-shaped cottage built on sloping land. Back then, it was adorned only with a pair of windowless black shutters pinpointing the whites of the wall like a set of eyes. Its body, wide at the front when viewed from the street and narrowing steadily at the back, gave the house the perpetually startled look of a structure either on the verge of falling face forward to its death or getting sucked into the void by the monsoon winds.

Property values in major cities have always been ridiculously high, but some of the most expensive real estate transactions in the world were recorded in Mumbai in the '90s. I dare say it was not so much the balmy weather or the stark beauty of the seascape but greed and foresight that drove every recently fattened entrepreneur to the little strip of land along the beach.

Within scarcely a decade, the chicken coop dwellings of scrawny fishermen, the airy, stucco fronts of chronic convalescents, the covered patios of retirees lounging on wicker chairs, and a grey, high walled missionaries' housing colony circling a children's playground -- throbbing with life and as much a part of the landscape as the jet black rocks that drew a jagged line between man and sea -- were all razed, and in their place, sterile fortresses of steel with form-follows-function architecture shot up like expletives.

And what of the natives? Many of them, including my parents, took the builders' cash and disappeared with their newfound wealth farther south where the cost of living was cheaper. A few opted for a flat in the newly constructed building instead of cash under-the-table, happy for the English style toilets and the doorman's desultory salute as one entered or exited the shiny new domicile.

Ami too opted for the flat, I suppose, and when I arrived at her doorstep, I was fairly certain, I was about to hear again all the grim and gory events of that horrific day when she signed away her heart, hashed and rehashed as much for me as for her own benefit.

I rang the doorbell and waited for what seemed like a long time before I heard the swish and sigh of fabric rubbing against legs. A maid answered and let me in. Smiling toothily, she said, "She is waiting for you." I followed, my heart hammering in my chest. I balled my fists and willed my mind not to register shock, dismay, pity, or any other expression that would cause her to retreat further into the darkness of despair.

"Saya."

"Ami."

She was stretched out on the bed, a sheet drawn tightly

across her body. If I was a little confused that she was lying down, though she expected company, I did not let on. I kissed her forehead and leaned back. She held my eyes for a long moment before her face squeezed into a ball of pain, and she wept silently. I held her close again, as her tears dampened her collar and the base of her neck.

"I love you."

"I love you too."

She pressed a buzzer on the wall beside her left arm. The maid came back in. She seemed to know what was expected, for she had a diaper, some lotion, and other unmentionables in her arms. Ami looked at me, asking me to wait outside, with her eyes.

"I'll hang out in your living room." I said and left at once. My throat hurt. I breathed in and out slowly. This is life, I said to myself. Grow up. After a few moments, I stopped shaking.

"You can go back in now," the maid said, making me jump out of my skin. I had retreated so far down memory's alleyways I actually had to look around to remind myself I was here with the new Ami. Ami the recluse. Ami halved and flung aside like an unusable appliance, a fork without tines, a hammer without claws.

"I'm sorry. I should have been prepared for your visit, but I fell asleep. I'm on these anti-depressants," she said by way of explanation. She was now seated on a chair, a shawl where her legs used to be.

"It's perfectly all right. May I switch on a light and part these curtains? If you sit in the light, you'll feel better." She nodded listlessly. The view from her window was breathtaking. The sea spread before us in sequined splendor. A sliver of light fell on Ami, cutting her face in two so that one half was in shadow, the other half luminous.

"You are so beautiful!" I blurted. It made her cry again.

"The last time someone said that to me was three years ago, before he headed abroad never to show his face again," she said, smiling through her tears.

I didn't say anything. The phone rang just then, and she picked it up on the second ring. I tried to shut out the one-sided conversation by leafing through a magazine and humming softly.

"Yes. No, not today. I have company. A dear friend. Girl, yes. Tomorrow, bye." She put the receiver back on the cradle.

"That was his father."

My eyes widened in disbelief.

"I know, Saya, you are wondering what I'm doing, sleeping with the enemy, figuratively speaking of course."

I shrugged, not meeting her eyes.

"You need to hear my story before you judge me."

"I wasn't," I began, but she cut me short.

"It's okay. You are not the only one. The whole world thinks I'm weird by now."

The maid came in with a glass of Coke resting on a saucer held up by a tray, the fizz not having the energy to make it to the top. A hunk of ice big as a glacier floated in the drink. She placed it carefully on a footstool by the bed and gestured I should have some. I nodded politely. She left the room, oddly turning the light switch off on her way out, but with the curtains parted, I realized I liked the view even better this way, just the two of us silhouetted against the setting sun waving an occasional wand of light over the ocean. Ami didn't seem to care one way or the other.

"My parents are simple, naive," she said without preamble, expecting me to tune in intuitively. "When the real estate boom happened, my father was ready to give up our home to the first builder who knocked on our door, for under five *lacs*. He had never seen so much money in his life. I bought train tickets for two and sent my parents to their village home until I'd figured out what we were going to do, if anything. Without my parents around, all the developers could do was give me some initial non-binding contracts to look over, suggesting I go over them carefully and make sure to get in touch soon."

Ami looked at me now with a smile in her voice. "You know how long I take to make even simple decisions, analyzing them to death. I remember, Saya, you'd tease me, 'It's either a samosa or a cheese fritter, Ami, not such a momentous decision you have to make the waiter stand behind your head for ten minutes!' I would hastily say, 'Samosa,' and then bite my tongue wishing I'd said cheese fritter."

I laughed out loud. I had to admit it was a fine imitation of the way we were, once upon a time. Me in a hurry and her hemming and hawing over every little thing.

Ami told me more:

> My head was spinning with all these options cloaked in legalese, the *hithertos, evidentiaries,* and *contingencies* that made no sense to me at all. Rather than say I did not understand the stuff that began jamming the door in thick brown envelopes over the weeks, I simply slid

it all in a drawer in my desk and hoped it would go away.

Then one day, my heart full of dark thoughts I dare not let surface, I went for my usual early morning walk and bumped into him, the man of my dreams. I just muttered, "Sorry," and went on, but he started walking with me. You know how conservative I am, Saya, along with being analytical. Normally, I'd have walked faster or brushed him off, but I happened to take a peek at those dimples in his rosy cheeks. Well, I was completely undone, as they say.

I should have used my common sense. Why would someone as devastatingly good-looking as Salim have anything to do with me? I was short, pudgy, and dark, like any girl next door. Yes, I had this mane and the dancers' eyes, but surely he could do better than me.

Well, he spent two months convincing me that we were made for each other. By the end of those two months, Saya, the mere mention of his name made my heart flutter like a bird, and I could not draw breath. Acute despair followed by euphoria, then fear, then anxiety became the new normal. I was an organism at war with itself, starved of some nutrients, overfed on others. Riddled with contradictions, my body was a vessel thirsty for his being. So he filled me. He told me he loved me over and over and over until, finally, one day, I was full. I believed him, and we began making plans. He wanted to study abroad and thought we should get married before he went away. I told him I would broach the subject with my parents when they return.

A trifle irritated, he asked me, "When would that be?"

I said, "Within a fortnight."

Hastily I called my parents and asked them to return at once. I sent them a money order, in case my father was not willing to return at the height of summer when tickets were most expensive. I was afraid he was beginning to enjoy the attentions of his ageing mother and the lizard-like pace of life.

Anyway, I could not annoy Salim. I watched his every expression like a hawk and stanched at the source the mere possibility of rebuke, so when he asked me a couple of days later to spend a weekend with him at a friend's bungalow, unoccupied at the time, I readily agreed. Of course, I had to close up the house and make provisions for my brothers to spend the weekend with a neighbor. Not wanting to become fodder for the gossips, I made up a complicated lie, telling her something about having to take care of an aunt who'd broken her hip and my parents not in town. Having knee and hip problems of her own, she took my brothers in, clicking her tongue in sympathy. Love makes a liar out of you, I suppose. Ours was and still is a society that does not condone promiscuity before marriage, but I believed I was lying for the sake of a greater truth, the truth about my feelings for Salim.

Indulge me for a bit, Saya, even though you might be embarrassed, for the memory of that one weekend allows me to live out the rest of my days here on earth tethered to my bed. I go over my tryst like a soft rag on mahogany taking pleasure in making it shine like a mirror.

We had to get to the bungalow separately for

obvious reasons. When I got there, it was eerily quiet and pitch dark, looming like a harbinger of doom in the mist, but it did not scare me one bit. On the contrary, I was very excited. I had always towed the line, Saya. Never missed a day of school, did my chores, homework, cared for my brothers, you know. I was being 'bad' for the first time in my life and was certain I could get away with it.

He opened the door before I even rang the doorbell and carried me in his arms to the bedroom without a word. I asked him if he didn't want to turn on a light and at least check out my new dress. He bit my neck and said, "What is the point?" He planned to tear it off anyway. And he did. Several times.

I cannot describe it as a beautiful or joyous or even tender experience. For one thing, I could not see his face or his maddening dimples although I did sense his smile from time to time. It was, to put it mildly, a night of passion – gritty, wild, and deeply satisfying.

It was still early, around 7 a.m. when I heard him whisper. I thought he was trying to rouse me. I opened my eyes. He was on the phone, but as soon as he saw me looking at him, he said, "It's done," and like a guilty school boy resumed his favorite sport, biting my neck and my ear and my ...

Well, we stayed in bed all that day and I left late in the evening when it was again too dark to be recognized, although I knew no one in that area. On the way home, following the lone star in the last bus speeding to the city, alone with my thoughts, the sweet ache in my limbs and the odor of debauchery clinging to my skin, I thanked my stars for his solicitous worrying about my reputation.

My parents came home on a Monday night. The next evening, their half-opened bags still sitting in the main room, we had a visit from Mr. Khan. He was a tall man, his back ramrod straight, his salt-and-pepper hair parted in the middle and smoothed down with gel. He had a wiry moustache, steel-rimmed glasses that glinted ominously in the sun, and a pair of shoes you could stare into to freshen your lipstick.

He was very courteous, very formal. He offered us a huge sum of money, unheard of in those days, and a very simple one-page contract. I was almost certain I would sign it and said, "I would sign it right now, except we don't do anything auspicious at this hour. Also, I want my lawyer to just give it a quick once over."

He stared hard at me, must have made up his mind that I was sincere, and said he could return in three days or three weeks, whenever it was convenient for me. I was impressed that he didn't force us into a corner and seemed so cool and collected about the deal. I said one week would be sufficient time, and could he come at 9 a.m., the auspicious hour? He stood up, shook my hand, patted my brother on his head, and left. My family was jubilant. My father would never have to work again. We could buy an apartment a little bit south of here in Santa Cruz and even afford a car. My brothers would go to college without having to take a loan! That was a Tuesday.

On Wednesday, I had another visitor. A Mr. Sood, a repulsive character with a big belly and a gold chain and his top buttons undone exposing his ape-like chest. I hated him. He kept licking his lips, so I gave him a drink. I thought he was thirsty. But no, it was just a nervous tic I guess. He offered us a couple of thousand more than Khan, but I wrote him off, at least mentally. So did my parents. They thought he was crude, sly, and probably ill intentioned. In any event, I told him we'd make a decision in a few days, and we'd call him. He had no documents with him but offered us some "holding" money and fairly insisted we keep the rather substantial bankroll even though I told him we didn't do business after sunset. When he left, I thrust the money into the same desk drawer with the other useless papers asking my brother to remind me to send it back to him in a couple of days.

The following day, Thursday, I came home from work to find Mr. Khan sitting in my living room with my mother standing around wringing her hands. I resented the fact that he had come uninvited, making my poor mother uncomfortable in her own home. I did not refrain from showing my annoyance. "Mr.

Khan, I thought we'd agreed I needed a week."

"I was just passing through and wondered if you have found a lawyer or need assistance with one," he said. That made sense, I suppose, but still, he didn't look his suave self that evening. He was drumming his fingers like a tradesman, and his forehead was damp.

"Thank you, I have a lawyer. We will be ready soon," I said coldly and stood up, forcing him to rise too. He was almost at the door when he said those foul words that destroyed my happiness.

Ami fell silent for nearly two minutes.

"What words?" I asked when I was beginning to think I would need to use her bathroom.

"He said, 'don't forget missy, you will be killing two birds with one stone if you take my offer'."

"What the heck did you mean by that?" I asked.

He said, "I meant, your family will have more money than they know what to do with, and you will have my son."

I did not know he had a son. Then I looked

closely at his hazel eyes behind those flinty glasses, his deep olive skin, and the beautifully arched brows and understood he was Salim's father and the best two months of my life were nothing but a lie, an entrapment of the most sordid kind.

"Get out!" I yelled.

"I will sell the house to Sood for a pittance, if I have to, but not to you. Never to you."

I will never forget the look in his eyes when he backed out of the room. We received a couple of calls that same evening. A strange voice that kept saying, "Be careful. Be careful" in a strangled sort of way, but I was too distraught to pay attention. Everyone gets crank calls sometimes, right? Now, thinking back, perhaps it was Salim. Perhaps not. I did not want to deal with *him* as yet.

What made Mr. Khan skittish enough to return to our home? Did he know I had another visitor the day after he made his offer? If so, how did he know? Did he have spies posted outside our door? It could've been the maid. Maybe she was hovering around when I accepted Sood's grimy little bankroll. Perhaps she was being bribed by Khan to keep a watch on our dealings. Don't look so surprised, Saya. This is prime property. If my home was worth *lacs* then, this apartment building that has risen out of its ashes is worth *crores* now, after just one decade. Every builder in Mumbai had the foresight to see that. I just did not recognize the lengths they would go to in order to obtain it. When it comes to wealth, Saya, there are no heroes, only villains in the making. Anyway, those were the questions I chose to torment myself with, knowing full well, were I to poke a stick in the muddy waters, a veritable geyser of pain would explode in my face.

Friday afternoon, I left a little earlier than usual, nursing a low-grade headache that made it hard to concentrate. I hadn't heard from Salim and wondered if we were done. Surely, even if he didn't love me, even if it had all been a ruse, surely I deserved one meeting, a shrug of an apology, a half-hearted word of regret?

I sedated myself with cough syrup for a few nights. The antihistamine put me promptly to sleep. But soon it became impossible to don high heels, work up a smile, and give a sales pitch eight hours a day every day of the week. So I took a mild sedative during the day as well and trudged on.

I got off the bus in a bit of fog and waited as I always did to cross the street. The light turned green. I took two steps, was lifted in the air, and the world as I knew it came to an end.

"Friday the thirteenth. A superstition come true for yours truly. Weird, isn't it?"

Great hacking sobs filled the room. I bent forward to comfort my friend and then realized it was I who was crying. Ami handed me my Coke, and I drank it at one gulp.

"Better?" she asked.

I nodded.

Saya, it was many afternoons later, filled only with the companionship of the slowly ticking clock, and a greasy, well-thumbed newspaper, that the truth struck me with a blow as savage as the one that struck my legs so that I actually saw one lifting in the air and heard the thud of the other that what happened to me on that fateful day was not an accident. It was a punishment. You see Sood and Khan were both fiercely competitive real estate moguls with many ties to the underworld. They both wanted our property the way the fat boy at a birthday party wants the biggest piece of the cake.

Khan dangled his son in front of me to obtain an edge, and I leaped like a bitch in heat. Then when I threw him out of the house, and he realized he had shown a severe lack of judgment with his "two birds with one stone'" remark, I was pushed under an oncoming truck. How ironic that both my parents and I thought Sood was the ill-intentioned party!

Anyway, the moment I understood, I called my parents and told them to sign the property over to Khan at once without wasting a second. They were confused, but as always, did what I asked.

"What! Why?" I shrieked horrified.

"Saya, I was not the only one they could hurt. I have two brothers. What if they were harmed next?"

I breathed in and out several times before I was calm again. Then I asked, "And *he* never came to the hospital? Not once?"

"A couple of days after I'd gained consciousness, Salim's sister came to see me with a bunch of red roses. She said he wanted to visit but was extremely traumatized. They had convinced him to stay home until he was calmer. She sat for a bit and then left. I watched from the glass panel on the door, as she spoke for a very long time to the doctor. I never saw her again, and apparently Salim never did recover from his trauma because he flew away. Out of sight, out of mind, I guess – his philosophy, not mine."

Again Ami sank into a silence as heavy as a tomb. The sky seemed suddenly darker as if the stars blew themselves out mourning her loss collectively.

"By the way, where is the rest of your family today? It's so quiet here."

"On vacation back in the village."

She read the look on my face. "I'm not completely alone, Saya. The nurse is here, and Khan comes over every evening."

"He does? Why?"

Ami explained:

The first time he showed up was at the hospital. I turned my face to the wall. He came again and again, and I did not relent. The sight of him made me want to set fire to the hospital, pull his heart out, and feed him to the dogs. But he kept showing up, and one day he stayed all day, until I finally turned my face and looked him in the eye.

"What do you want from us? You have your signed document," I muttered.

"I want to apologize. I wanted them to scare you, not throw you under the truck," he said and began to weep. When he was done, I told him they had succeeded in scaring me, and then some, so he could bugger off. He would not get forgiveness from me. "And while you are at it, throw yourself under a truck," I screamed at his back.

Still, he came over every day. My parents told me he was covering all the hospital costs and later when they took me to a fancy rehabilitation center, that cost was covered by him too. I did not thank him. When our house was razed and the building ready, I was brought to this flat. It has a ramp and the entire place is designed with my needs in mind. The apartment was not part of the original contract. I guess this was payment for my emotional and physical distress. I still did not thank him. He asked me one day, quite humbly, if it pleased me: the apartment, the furnishings, and the round-the-clock care.

I told him to bugger off, of course. Then I said, "If you can give me back my legs for one hour, just one hour so that I can bury my feet in the warm sand and feel the water tickling my toes, so that I can stand at eye level with the world, so I can bend and stretch and dance the rumba, so I can wear a sari, so I can walk to the kitchen for a glass of water and run to the store for a loaf of bread, so I can wash my own backside without a nurse smelling my humiliations, so I can wipe the merciless pity from the faces of this earth... if you can give me that for an hour, I will forgive you."

He's never asked me that question again. Still he came over, every day, rain or shine until his wife thought he was some sort of a pervert and his daughter called and asked me to discourage him from seeing us so often, for his 'interest' in me was disrupting their family life. I told her, you guessed it, to bugger off too. I would do whatever I desired from this throne in my prison.

There wasn't much we had in common, so at first he just hung about looking forlorn. Then one day he brought a carom board, and we played for a while, and the ticking of the clock stopped torturing me for a bit. A few weeks later, he brought a pack of cards and began teaching me how to play bridge, and now oftentimes we play chess. I still do not thank him. And neither does he expect it anymore. He just enjoys my company, and I think, even finds this neighborhood frog kind of pretty!

"I wish you wouldn't keep putting yourself down. You are pretty and smart and have a great deal of spunk," I said.

"I am broken," she said in a small voice, "but thank you."

"He never mentions his son?" I couldn't help asking. "I find it hard to believe he did not love you. The fact that you spent a weekend together had to have meant something, wouldn't it, and…"

"And what?" she asked.

"I remember you said, that morning at the bungalow, you heard him talk over the phone. He hung up the moment you woke up and gave you his full attention. Well, if he did not care about you, he wouldn't be that solicitous, would he?"

She stared thoughtfully out of the window. It was pitch dark, and after her story about being pushed under the truck, I was still a little spooked.

"Saya," she said, "why don't you stay the night? It will be so much fun. I haven't had a girls' night in three years."

"Okay," I agreed at once.

"To answer your question, yes I thought for a long time about that. Perhaps it was cowardice that kept him away from the hospital, and later his family convinced him to move away. I can almost hear their argument: what was the point of tying the knot with a woman who would only tag along with him like an apology for the rest of his life? He was young. He had his life ahead of him, but there was something *else* that was niggling at me like the cramps in my legs long after they were cut off. I finally asked Khan about it."

"What?" I asked, anxiously.

"The morning after our ... umm ... frenetic 'honeymoon' night when Salim saw me awake he said two words, 'It's done.' At the time I thought he mouthed those words to me, *after* he'd disconnected, suggesting he was done with the conversation and could devote himself to me, but that interpretation was untrue, an illusion of memory. You see, hung over from love, I believed what I wanted to believe. The truth is he was saying those words into the phone to the person at the other end."

I frowned, perplexed.

"Don't you get it? When our relationship progressed from deep revulsion to remote tolerance and throttled conversations, putting aside the last ounce of my pride, I asked Khan to do me a favor. He looked up like a dog salivating and wagging his tail, 'Sure thing. What can I do?' he asked. I told him to go check his phone records. Let me know if his son called him on a specific weekend in October at 7.30 a.m. or thereabouts and spoke with him for under two minutes. He came back the next day, and said, indeed he had. I don't think he realized how easily he'd implicated himself."

"I don't believe it!"

"It's true, Saya, his father asked him to seduce me, do whatever it took so that I would be putty in his hands when it came to signing the papers, and Salim obliged. When it was over, he called his pop and said exactly that: it's done. Then riddled with belated guilt, he screwed me again."

I couldn't breathe. Nor, I realized, could I stay with her that night. I would not have been very good company. Ami's life had been ripped apart, and I knew she was trying to put some of the pieces back as best as she could. But Khan had made his insidious way back into her life selfish in his need for forgiveness, and although she claimed never to have forgiven him, she still let him into her life. I could not reconcile myself with that. I wanted to go home and have time to process everything I'd just heard.

I was almost out the door when I realized I'd left my pocketbook on the floor beside her bed. A little light from the hallway shone on her face. She was sitting still, tracing a delicate finger over an old black and white photograph. I did not want to intrude and tiptoed in to retrieve my stuff.

"You look so much like your father, Salim," she whispered.

A wave of comprehension followed by a flood of pity held me rooted to the spot, my one hand extended. Now her eyes were on me, but looking beyond at the ghost of

Salim. I raced out of the apartment my pocketbook tap tapping on my legs and headed instinctively towards the water.

Waves danced on the ocean their crystalline dance. The moon and all the heavenly bodies shook their fingers in ire; a sudden burst of rain, a clap of lightning, and a parting of clouds illuminated the scene like the flash of a camera. I found shelter under the only remaining canopied bus stop, hugging my drenched body, my teeth chattering as much from the deluge as from what I'd inadvertently witnessed.

Saturated with a sense of doom, the very next day I told my mother I was cutting my visit short. I also told her I was glad she'd sold our sea-face home and moved away. The ocean is evil. It snatches men's souls. She looked at me strangely and pressed a cool palm to my burning forehead.

In time, I hoped the restful whistling of the goldfinch, the gentle dropping of snow on rooftops, and the sudden flowering of the pear tree outside my bedroom window in New Jersey would erase from memory the waves grappling with their ambivalence toward the shore, and save only the one who counts each infernal rise and ebb unmoving from her ocean-front property. ♦

A Murder

For who goes up your winding stair
can ne'er come down again…

- Mary Howitt
("The Spider and the Fly," 1829)

I call my mother once a week, and if I ever neglect to do so, she doesn't complain, allowing a pained silence to get her message across instead. So to be woken in the middle of the night by the ringing of the phone and the tediously long number on the Caller ID suggesting it is from India is nothing short of jarring.

"Hello." My whisper, padded with anxiety, wakes my

husband.

"Saya, Saya. It's me, Mum."

"Mmm. Is everything all right? It's the middle of the night."

"I am fine, but a terrible thing has happened. A nightmare thing. Terrible."

I can sense her trembling. I sit up fully, miming to my husband to turn on the light and mouthing, "It's my mum."

"What is it? Is someone sick? Accident?" I ask.

"It's Maina, you know the upstairs…"

"Of course, I know Maina. What's wrong with her?"

"She's dead! Someone slashed her neck!"

I truly thought my mother was hallucinating, but her sobbing suggested otherwise. Then just as suddenly, she stopped.

"Oh, it is the middle of the night there," she wailed. "I'm sorry. I will call you at daybreak."

"What? No! I'm fully awake now."

But she'd already hung up on me, another one of those infuriating old people habits one cannot get upset about because we know they don't mean to be rude.

Putting the receiver slowly back on the cradle, the full force of her words finally sinking in, I rose with a little shriek, headed to the washroom, and hurled the contents of my dinner in the bowl. Then groaning at the taste of bile in my mouth, I brushed my teeth, washed my face, and went downstairs to the kitchen, waving at my husband to get back into bed, as I prepared myself for a bleak night of stale Oreos, anxiety, and copious tears.

At 8 a.m., long past "daybreak" in Mum's words, and accounting for the time difference, about 6.30 p.m. in Mumbai, I called her. She answered at the first ring.

"Now tell me what's going on, and don't worry about my phone bill; it's free for me," I lied.

She took a deep sigh, and I assume, settled on the sofa beside the phone table.

"I will miss her so much … so much…she was a real daughter to me."

I felt a pang of jealousy. I was my mother's only daughter. However, while I lived across an ocean, Maina was the one who had been by her side through good times and bad, and of course, I was infinitely grateful for that. Nevertheless, her choice of words …I shook myself. This was no time for recrimination.

"What exactly happened, Mama?"

She said, "It was about 4 p.m., and Maina must have been resting. It is excruciatingly hot in Mumbai right now, and you know we are all used to our little siesta before teatime.

Apparently the watchman announced that two boys wished to visit her. They held a packet of sweets and a large red envelope, the kind used for wedding invitations, in their hands. I don't know if she asked the watchman any questions. I think she simply told him to send them up. Maina is, <u>was</u> a trusting soul. Often, she worried me with her optimism, her belief that people were essentially good, and if you put your best smile forward, the world would receive you with open arms. I chided her now and then, but not forcefully. I was aware that she was young. Life had not soured her, and a part of me was loath to destroy her illusions. I thought, who knows, maybe I'm the one who is wrong. Maybe my own disposition attracts misfortune like flies to refuse. Now, I wish I had warned her to check and double check the locks at night, not give out too much

> information to strangers, and all the other commonsense advice at my disposal. She would have listened, out of respect, I'm sure. On the other hand, she has ... she had... a loving husband, home each night to keep her safe. Maybe that's why I did not say much.

"There is nothing you can do or say to prevent monsters from committing senseless, random crimes, Mum. It's not your fault," I said.

> "From what I've gathered, it was not a random act of terror. Of course, we can only deduce what may have happened from the evidence discovered by her husband Jai and the police. Jai told me everything in a voice so calm I knew he had to be in deep shock. He said he always texted his wife before leaving work. That evening he texted her a couple of times asking her not to cook dinner, that perhaps he could make it home earlier than usual. They would walk along the beach and eat the spicy street food she loved so much, but she did not respond to his texts. Then he called her, and she did not answer or phone him back. He finally called her on her cell phone, but his messages

went into voicemail. He was truly concerned. It was not like Maina to ignore his messages, and if she had a salon or a medical appointment, she generally let him know before he left for work. It's an hour's drive from his office, but he made it in thirty-five minutes, he said. He rang the doorbell and then opened the door with his own key."

Mum was crying now. Her soft anguished mewling made my heart race, and my hands grew so clammy that I dropped the phone. I picked it up hastily, afraid I might have disconnected. I hadn't. Her shudders were so palpable, my arms automatically opened to give her a hug. When she calmed a bit, she told me what Jai found:

> There were two glasses of orange sherbet untouched on the coffee table and a pool of blood so thick, Jai was screaming long before he saw her. Even before he got to the kitchen, the cuffs of his trousers were soaked in blood like the stains from betel juice. She was stretched out under the breakfast table, the chairs topsy-turvy, her neck slashed with a butcher blade, her jaw raised heavenward and the whites of her eyes already tracing the afterworld.

On the stove was a fry pan, the gas turned off. In the fry pan, a batch of onion fritters floated drunkenly in oil, obviously meant for her honored guests when they surprised her in the kitchen and committed the heinous act.

Why? The oldest reason in the world. Greed. Cash, jewelry, and some silver went missing from her bedroom cupboard, things that they could hide in their pockets before they brazenly walked out the door. Although the watchman had seen the two young men, and the police questioned him for hours, he said he didn't find them menacing, only a little bedraggled like someone's poor cousins from the village. Later, he was very certain, he said he had seen Maina's son hanging about with them a couple of years ago at the local sandwich shop and a few hole in the wall stalls selling cigarettes, bottled water, other things that have mushroomed in the neighborhood.

Her son! I'd forgotten she had one. "Where is her son now, Mum?"

"On his way down from London where he works as a hot shot investment banker."

I smiled in spite of myself. I doubted that my mum knew what an investment banker did, smart as she was. She was obviously repeating neighborhood gossip.

Mum said, "I cannot understand why her son would choose the company of two obviously ignorant, evil, impoverished men though. He was a smart college boy, headed for Europe. I just don't understand it. But that is why I don't think it was a random act, Saya. These boys knew her house, the floor plan, probably her habit of keeping cash lying about from associating with her son."

Mum sounded as if she had aged overnight. Her voice had a little tremble, as if the words were being pushed through a pitifully corroded pipe, and the sound made my heart sink. My mother was supposed to live forever. Without her ... I shook off my fears.

"Get some rest, Mum. I'll call you tomorrow, same time. I have to make breakf..." She hung up before I could finish the sentence. Nothing was going to come between her daughter and her son-in-law's omelet.

Later that day, as I sat down to yet another solitary cup of tea, my instinct was to call Maina, as I'd often done in the past. "Check on Mum, will you? She didn't sound good on the phone," I wanted to tell her. The fact that Mum was grieving the loss of the only woman who could comfort her in her time of need struck me afresh, and for a long while I sat there stunned and a little disoriented.

From my vague and troubled ruminations appeared Maina's smiling face, the teeth white and even, the cheeks always a tad rosy from her favorite blush-on, her hair braided loosely as she strode in at all hours of the day with the ease of a well loved friend to show off a new sari or share a dessert. She ran up and down from her floor to ours, so I remember her as always sounding a little breathless. One day she rang the doorbell repeatedly, and hopping from foot to foot, her hands damp and yellow with gram flour, she asked Mum if it was okay to put cumin in eggplant fritters because she'd already done so and could she please tell her quick because her oil was bubbling in the pan. For some reason, Mum had found the situation extremely funny and could barely nod her response, she was laughing so hard. Then Maina laughed as well, and soon we were all giggling hysterically, for no apparent reason. When she left, bits of gram flour dribbling from her fingers dotted the floor giving cause for more merriment.

Mum had lost a "daughter" and a friend in Maina, and sitting on my couch in New Jersey with the memory of laughter tinkling in my veins, time crashed into distance and I had what I can only describe as a discombobulated moment so that I began opening all the doors of my house confusing it with Mum's apartment, trying to locate the front door that led to the floor above where Maina was inexplicably hiding.

I wasn't always close to Maina. At first, I looked forward to her unscheduled visits only so that I could leave the house with clear conscience for an hour or two.

'Mum was in good hands,' I said to myself, "and probably preferred getting a little time off from her cantankerous daughter."

Then one day, I returned home to find Maina sitting quietly by herself as Mum napped in the other room.

"I thought I'd wait till you returned. Her BP is a little high. I asked her to rest."

Guilt made me defensive. "Well, I was only gone for an hour," I said. "You could leave now, if you like."

Maina did not say anything. She simply took my hand and clasped it in both of hers. I suppose that was the moment we became sisters.

Once, Mum was invited to a lunch and movie by her 'sister network'. She wanted me to come along. I declined, saying I had a few errands to run. After she left, Maina made one of her unannounced visits. "Are you busy?" she asked.

"Nothing that cannot wait," I said, and we got comfortable. I don't know at what point she began talking about herself, but when she finished, I knew I was in the presence of an extraordinary person. She touched me deeply, and now that she was gone, I'm amazed I recalled her words so precisely.

"Saya, did you know I had no roof over my head until the age of two? Yes, I was the one of those snot-nosed little beggars with the unhealthy potbelly you see in UNICEF commercials. Then one day I was picked up, quite literally, by a social worker. For many years, I fantasized about this man, ascribing him with God-like qualities. It was only recently when I saw a documentary on baby sellers that it occurred to me he may have been just a man after all, looking to make a buck off some very vulnerable people. He carried me in his arms and through a series of clever maneuvers, creating false birth and medical records and then enlisting me with an adoption agency was able to 'legitimately' hand me to a couple he knew was looking for a girl child of about two years and of fair coloring, a Mr. and Mrs. Batra."

She stopped to catch a breath and noted the stricken look on my face, "I'm sorry. Am I embarrassing you Saya?"

"No. Of course not. I'm just…this is unexpected. I just thought…"

"You thought I was like you and everybody else in this building. A girl with a normal background. Parents who loved me, nurtured me, gave me an education, allowed me to dream," she said with a rueful smile.

I shrugged, "Yes."

"Well, it wasn't what happened. The Batras were kind to me, but my adoptive father never let his wife forget she had not borne him any children. He played around, drank excessively, and finally became one of those low-life wife batterers." She stopped and stared at me hard.

"Do you want to know what happened next?"

I nodded like one in a dream.

"Mrs. Batra set fire to herself."

Maina ignored my squeal of terror.

"It seemed to be the trend in the seventies and eighties. There were numerous articles in the paper about dowry-deaths where vulture hungry in-laws, dissatisfied with the girl's meager possessions, reduced her to cinders as easily as burning dead grass. I know. I've done a lot of reading on the subject. Anyway, I assume that was her exit plan."

"And Mr. Batra?" I asked faintly.

"Oh, he tried to save her and got pulled into the pyre as well."

I gulped. How casually Maina told her story, I thought at the time. Now, I realize, perhaps the only way to deal with trauma of this sort is to distance oneself from it and become an observer. Then I wondered if she was perhaps pranking me? Was this her idea of a pleasant afternoon in the company of friends? I looked at her, almost pleading. Say it wasn't so, I begged mutely. But she went on.

"The Batras were not celebrities. Their story was trite. A family drama that made yesterday's headlines. By the end of the week, I was forgotten," Maina said and incredibly, began rocking herself and singing, *down will come baby, cradle and all.*

The back of my neck was damp. "Who raised you?" I asked. My hands were tented as in prayer, and I settled in to hear the rest of Maina's story.

> "I was raised by the ayah Miriam Ma who they hired almost the same day I was adopted. She took me home. I lived in her hutment for the next ten years. Yes, Saya. A hut. My roof was a piece of tarp. My bedding was newspaper from

the trash. My lullabies were the snores of drunken neighbors I could touch through my muslin walls. My dinner came specially catered by the five-star garbage can behind the Taj Hotel. I didn't mind any of it though. Neither did my stomach – ironclad to this day.

Miriam treated me like an equal. I was assigned tasks I could handle. I was punished without violence and rewarded without hugs. She admired women of strength and took me to see movies about goddesses and queens and warrior women. She despised tears.

"If the poor resorted to tears, the rivers would get flooded, and we can't have that, now can we?"

That was her favorite dialog. But most importantly, she had the foresight to steal enough from the Batra household, before their relatives came to collect their ashes and their possessions, that I may get an education. That's how I became the most educated and envied girl in the slums. For my high school graduation, she bought me a transistor radio. When I received my degree in history and

> economics, she gave me ten thousand rupees and said her job was done. I needed to move out of the slums and make a life for myself. My little friends all ended up as either servants in households such as these we now live in, or they began selling their bodies for bread.

I tried to suppress another squeal by pretending to cough into my shirtsleeve.

"How…where…did you meet your husband?" I asked, hoping against hope her answer would not shock, dismay or frighten me. I had had enough for one day.

She laughed. "That's quite a story in itself," she said, making my heart sink.

> "Jai's parents are the ultimate snobs. I was a mere receptionist at Warner's, living in the women's hostel on the wrong side of town. He already had an office and an administrative assistant and was on a pretty fast track. But he fell in love with me. To this day, and we've been married twelve years, his parents like to tell the story of how we met, implying we were colleagues rivaling for the same position in the company and that I did not really need to work and did so only because I enjoyed the

intellectual challenge. Ha! I've come this close to telling them and their idiot friends to take their intellectual challenge and put it you know where. But I love Jai, you see.

"Anyway, when they suggested they'd like to meet me formally 'in my own setting' so that they could judge my socio-economic status I suppose, I had to resort to some pretty wild shenanigans.

"Miriam Ma was still a servant, in another household by then. I told her about Jai's parents and how they expected their future daughter-in-law to be as priggish and uppity as them. With a cunning that came as naturally as adding water to increase the volume of milk, she came up with a plan.

"She asked me to invite his parents over to her place of work on a Friday evening. That was when, like clockwork, her boss and his madam went out to dinner and the movies. In essence, I invited Jai's folk over to a stranger's home for tea. As a result, Miriam was able to meet them as well. It all went perfectly. They were quite impressed."

"But you couldn't have put wool over their eyes forever! I'm sure in time…"

"In time, I made up another story. Most people are too self-absorbed to pay too much attention to anything that does not affect their comfort, Saya," Maina said, continuing.

> "We had a yearlong engagement, and before we were married, I told them I was renting another place, then another, and would not buy one until I was satisfied with the address, the view, the club in the vicinity, etc. Their esteem for me increased exponentially, trust me. They even forgave me the fact that I was an orphan and in all likelihood have fabricated some heartrending story even about that to circulate amongst friends.
>
> "Jai knew everything about me of course, and did not mind because he loved me!"

LOVED ME! LOVED ME! LOVED ME! Maina's words reverberated now near, now far until I pulled myself together with an effort.

Mum sounded stronger the next day. "Saya," she said without preamble, "they caught the men who hurt … who killed Maina."

"The two men? How?"

"They lacked both morals and brains I suppose," she said dryly. "Listen. It's all in the papers. Let me read it out to you:

MUMBAI TIMES: The police have solved the murder of Maina Sahni (48), whose body was found in a pool of blood by her husband in their 10th floor flat in Mirabel building, Worli, on Tuesday night. The police arrested two men known to the victim's family, who have confessed that they murdered her for money.

"The police found a cell phone among a pile of kitchen utensils, pans, knives and ladles in an oversized trash can." Mum continued without catching her breath. "They believe one of them must have swept everything on the counter on to the bin when lunging across to hold her still as she groped for something, a knife, a rolling pin, anything to protect herself. Her fingerprints were all over the surface of the counter indicating that she fought and writhed in agony. His cell phone probably fell out of his breast pocket. I believe there were over fifty text messages to his accomplice, clearly mentioning the intent to murder, the time, the method, and every other incriminating bit of evidence one can conceive. They traced the cell phone to the source and found the man who owned it. He did not waste any time ratting on his partner either."

"Oh, Mummy, poor, poor Maina!"

"Yes. I will never forget her. I have told her husband he must dine with us one day a week for the rest of his life. I wish to keep her memory alive forever," Mum said with exhaustion in her voice, and hung up.

As to whether my mum followed through on her dinner invitation, I do not know. The last time I asked, Maina's husband had left that apartment and moved to another State. We did not hear from him again. It was Maina who drew us all together in her "claw hitch" knot. When we lost her, the knot loosened on its own accord, and we drifted apart. My beautiful Mum passed away a few months later. Perhaps Maina's death had something to do with her demise. Or perhaps she just grew weary of mending the same old heart. ♦

An Explanatory Note

She was the third child from my grandfather's first marriage, and I am her third child, an only daughter. Now my mother is gone. I trace my fingers over her face in family albums and in a fit of inspiration gather our conversations like temple flowers and weave them into a garland.

This is a work of fiction. The story of my mother's childhood, her entry into my father's world after marriage, the fact that she raised his brother and two sisters, as well as us children, however are all true. They gleam like diamonds and need no embellishment.

Other stories of relatives who have passed on or disappeared from our lives decades ago are speckled with memory loss and the confusion that comes from having a family as large as a small village. In an effort to keep you engaged, for what storyteller can resist a captive audience, I have taken the liberty to cover those holes with a fistful of drama.

Still others are purely the products of my overactive mind: snatches of conversations with school friends, local color gathered like sea salt in the hem of my skirt, and bits of news heard on Mum's old-fashioned radio on those annual visits home.

It is my fervent hope that you will see these stories as you would the stuff of dreams. In other words, concern yourself not so much with the scenarios but the way they made you feel upon waking - those ordinary characters, who passed briefly through my life but stayed with me like an oft-remembered fragrance.

Liberally sprinkled throughout the book are the expressions, attitudes, and affectations of various aunts, cousins, and friends. I think Mum would appreciate this collision of life with art, but still she would want to keep their privacy intact, which is why I have changed their names and locations.

Finally, take these offerings with a pinch of salt, dear reader, for this is how I hold on to my mother and to a way of life. ♦

A Word of Thanks

Thank you to all those who arrived in my life as guests, and stayed as precious memories. Without you I would be at a loss for words. And these stories would not be told.

Thank you early readers. Your encouragement urged me on.

Thank you Chandrakant Seth for your invaluable help with cover design.

Thank you to the men in my life – my husband Deepak, my children Sugreev and Pranav. You are my wealth. ♦

About the Author

Poonam Chawla was born and educated in Mumbai where she held a prominent position as a copywriter in an ad agency before she moved to USA and began a new career in the corporate arena. She resides in New Jersey with her husband of thirty-three years and two loving children. This is her second book. ♦

Also By P. A. Chawla

The Shenanigans of Time

An absorbing, vivid look at Indian culture ... Chawla, in her debut, portrays well-rounded characters whose different points of view usefully inform the collection as a whole. The author understands how families challenge and sustain their members ... "And father and son plucked an hour out of time, to be savored then stored in the cool, dark cellar of memory marked Private Reserve."

- Kirkus Reviews

A very interesting read. P.A Chawla puts together a series of interconnected short stories in an almost cinematic way, like an Inarritu movie in which different families of immigrants are bound by a common fate. Chawla gives another dimension to what it means to be a "Desi" in the United States. The lives they leave behind in India, the relationship between the old and new generations and other cultural differences make this a unique collection of stories.

- Amazon Review

In her first collection of interlocking stories, P. A. Chawla reveals myriad emotions – the turmoil and transcendence of childhood, parenthood, sex and love –

that shapes the ordinary mind. Whether it is the motelier Deven Shah and his deep seated desire to be embraced as the quintessential local only to be regarded as a foreigner by his only child, or Saya Sharma who fades in and out of her suburban life like a migratory bird, or the visiting Feroz grasping for a chance at domesticity with the volatile Rita, The Shenanigans of Time is a hymn of praise for the resilience of the human spirit and the desire for a place to call home. ♦

CPSIA information can be obtained
at www.ICGtesting.com
Printed in the USA
FFOW04n2035261015
17966FF